SCALLON'S LAW

by

Elliot Long

Dales Large Print Books
Long Preston, North Yorkshire,
BD23 4ND, England.

British Library Cataloguing in Publication Data.

Long, Elliot
    Scallon's Law.

A catalogue record of this book is
available from the British Library

ISBN   1-84137-007-X pbk

First published in Great Britain by Robert Hale Ltd., 1999

Cover illustration © Faba by arrangement with Norma Editorial

Published in Large Print 2000 by arrangement with Robert Hale Ltd.

Dales Large Print is an imprint of Library Magna Books Ltd.

Printed and bound in Great Britain by
T.J. (International) Ltd., Cornwall, PL28 8RW

ONE

Luke Scallon stepped tiredly down off his big roan and wrapped the reins around the tie rail. The jangling of the piano coming from the rundown saloon he stood in front of jarred on his ears. The legend on the board above it told him it was John's Place. And his thoughts about the din matched his already ragged disposition. He even wondered why in the hell didn't somebody do something about tuning the damned instrument. It'd help.

He scrubbed his week-old stubble and blinked lids over steely eyes, which were sunk into dark shadows, due to lack of sleep. His mood was sombre. He didn't like towns. They usually spelt trouble. And as well as being tired, he was hungry. He was also as irritated as a stag during the rut at having been fooled by Ben Hagler back there in those rain-soaked mountains.

Trying to shake himself out of his black mood he squared his wide shoulders and dragged his Winchester from its saddle scabbard. Then, purposefully, he stepped up on to the boardwalk and strode across it on scuffed-up saddle boots.

Inside, he found the saloon was busy. The stuffy warmth, along with the smell of booze and tobacco smoke, hit him like a smack in the face after the pure, high-altitude air he'd been breathing for the past week.

The place was alive with conversation, too – some rowdy, some quiet. That was another thing he'd not been used to lately. Talk. Man talk, anyway. This past week there'd only been the song of birds to listen to – the solitary scream of eagles, the hoot of owls, the lonely, spine-tingling night chorus of the wolves and the yapping of coyotes, but, towards the end, even they had got to be tiresome, though they usually didn't bother him.

So damn Ben Hagler, for he did!

Made sour by the reminder he stepped across the saloon floor. At the long mahogany bar he set his rifle against the scarred wood and placed a boot on the brass foot-rail.

He eyed the diminutive 'keeper. 'You got any beer?'

'Sure.' The barman dropped the wipe he had been using over his shoulder. 'Comin' right up.'

When the amber brew arrived Scallon paid up and took the top off it. Though warm, he found it was of passable quality. But it irked him slightly to have the small 'keeper stay on and look expectantly at him while he drank.

After moments the barman said, enthusiastically, 'Shipped in from Cheyenne every week.'

Scallon stared. 'You want a medal fer that?'

The 'keeper's brown eyes, set in a saloon-pallored, hollow face, dulled. He said. 'Jest thought you'd like to know.'

Scallon scowled. 'Well, I don't. Now ... you serve food?'

Though clearly disappointed, the 'keeper said, 'Why, sure. Every day, all day. But right now you've hit a bad time. Just two hours ago the cook went sick with the stomach ache. Boss ain't got a replacement yet.' Then he grinned, as if to make one last effort to strike up some sort of rapport. 'Guess he must have tried his own slop,' he chirped cheerfully.

But, Scallon found, even that didn't dent his tetchiness. He just stared, stonily. 'An' you figure that funny, huh?'

Obviously despairing now, the barkeeper shrugged. 'Well, can't say I didn't try,' he said. He waved an arm at the wide, sun-blasted street outside. 'There's Jenny Manners' place, a-ways up from here,' he said, 'she....'

'Charlie!' The roar came from the other end of the bar. 'We gittin' any service here?'

Scallon's swift, hard glance in the

direction of the bellow told him it had come from an impatient, bearded man waving a glass. For a moment he thought it could have been Hagler, but it wasn't. Scallon allowed himself to relax. He returned his gaze to the barman.

He wasn't surprised to see the 'keep appeared to be glad of the opportunity to move and mingle with more buoyant company than he was now engaged with, for he was hollering, 'Comin' right up, Herb.' Nevertheless, he paused long enough to fully search Scallon's hard, bony features with his brown gaze. His glance immediately showed a hint of alarm. Scallon knew his scarred face and the cold, grey, lack of emotion in his watchful eyes could inspire that effect in some men.

Now clearly in a hurry to get away the 'keeper said hastily, 'Believe me, mister, Jenny Manners serves the best steaks in town. I eat there myself.'

Feeling slightly mollified by Charlie's continued efforts to be social, Scallon said,

'Well, I thank you for that, man.'

Charlie nodded, relaxed, said, ''Tain't nothin',' and scuttled off.

The news of the eatery under his belt, Scallon drained the last of the beer in the glass and reached for his rifle.

It was as he stooped for it that he saw the batwing doors swing open. They were being pushed apart by a burly, unkempt man wearing a brown, open duster which covered his dark-grey, muddied suit. A gunbelt and holster hung around his ample waist. The man's dirty black hat was tipped forward, as if it had been shading his wary gaze. His strong, aggressive jaw jutted out from under the shadow of its wide brim. Scallon estimated there must be at least a week's growth of beard on his face ... much like there was on his own chin.

And, no doubt about it – It was Ben Hagler.

Scallon watched the mixture of dread and disbelief come to Ben's black, searching glare as it tangled his own steely gaze.

Recognition by both was immediate. With a startled gasp, Hagler scrambled back, out on to the boardwalk. As he went, he clawed for his Colt. The batwings flapped briskly to, hiding him.

Then the boom of Hagler's Colt – poked above the batwings – set a lot of things hurrying into motion. Startled yells filled the stifling air of the saloon. Chairs rattled back, bodies went to floorboards, or behind upturned tables.

Scallon hunched forward into a mean crouch. A leonine smile formed a snarling curve on his cruel lips. He felt the pluck of Hagler's lead as it passed through the green shirt-wool covering his right arm. He triggered the Winchester, which he now had clamped against his right hip. He saw his lead smash a splintering path through the lower door-slats.

As he jacked in another load, more lead came his way from the boardwalk. He felt it fan his cheek. Its heat was harsh and sudden. But the yell of pain that came from beyond the batwings told him his own first shot had struck home and Hagler was now trying to buy himself some time.

Still crouched against the bar, Scallon pressed the rifle's trigger once more. Again his lead savaged the flimsy batwings. Over their now quivering tops he could see Hagler was retreating, groaning and limping, across the boardwalk before hopping down on to the street. The sight of Hagler's distress caused Scallon's hard stare to gleam with grim contentment.

So he had hit the bastard.

Mean-faced he straightened, jacked in another load and paced across the floor. But at the batwings he paused. There'd be no taking chances here. Hagler was poison in any man's language and not to be trifled with.

It was only when Scallon heard the beat of hooves on the sun-baked main street outside and saw Hagler spurring his unkempt mount up the strip, that he let his natural instincts for prudence go out of the window. He wanted Hagler alive – or the authorities at Rutland did, the county seat, who were part paying for this manhunt.

Bounding out on to the street, Scallon saw Hagler had only got fifty yards up the track before he'd been halted. Across his path was a large freight wagon, the twelve mules hauling it seemingly frightened by the sudden roar of gunfire. They were thrashing and straining against the traces. Then Scallon saw the blood glistening redly on Hagler's right thigh. And he could hear Hagler was shouting raucously at the cursing, red-faced driver who was fighting the startled beasts.

This time Scallon was deliberate. He focused the bead of the rifle's sight on the outlaw. He was not in the least distracted by the scattering, alarmed people moving to get out of the line of fire, or the maddened bucking and jostling of the freight team. Indeed, he found a certain amount of satisfaction in the situation. God must be on his side. He'd honestly thought Hagler had out-schemed him back there in the mountains and he'd lost him. It seems fate had decreed otherwise, had dropped the owlhoot right in his lap and was now holding him there.

'Stay real still, Hagler!' he bawled. 'I got you dead to rights.'

The owlhoot swung around, his stare wild and desperate. Then he roared, 'Go to hell, Scallon!' He swung up his Colt and fired.

While Hagler's lead hummed past him, Scallon answered. The boom of his rifle thundered angrily above the other noises. He had the satisfaction of seeing Hagler spread his arms, see his Colt fly out of his hand. The owlhoot was giving out with a despairing yell as he toppled out of the saddle. When he hit the ground he lay like a sack of potatoes, face down on the dusty street.

Scallon straightened alertly, his hunter's instincts honed to knife-edge keenness. He was not distracted by the big freight wagon that was now careering wildly past him, churning up acrid dust. The mules were still only half under control, the driver still wrestling with the traces and cursing blue lights as he strove to bring the team to full order. Hagler's bay began running with the mules, its eyes wild, stirrups flapping.

Not fazed by the commotion, Scallon gazed at Hagler. The owlhoot's stillness puzzled him. In his long experience, Scallon had got to know there was usually *some* threshing movement from a hit man. He'd aimed to disable Hagler, not kill him, and he thought he'd done that.

So, for moments, he stared suspiciously at the owlhoot. Hagler looked dead, and, if he was, that was unfortunate. Even so, Scallon remained wary. Once before he had been hoodwinked by a gun-toting sonofabitch playing possum. The result had put him on his back for a week, near to death, and had left him having to carry the scars for the rest of his life.

He stepped forward cautiously, rifle held ready. He was oblivious to the heat of the sun beating down on his big shoulders. He was unaware of the white faces now peering from windows and doorways each side of him. The rumble of the runaway freight wagon was now an unheeded, fading din in the distance. It was the woman's shout from the boardwalk to his right that startled him.

'What are you going to do?' she demanded.

He didn't look her way, kept his eyes riveted on Hagler. He said, 'It'll be up to him, ma'am.'

He walked on. He was near up to Hagler before the outlaw made his play. Abruptly, he flipped over. Hate filled his black stare as he gazed up. And as he rolled Scallon saw the small Colt sixshooter he'd dug out from some hidden place in his clothing. It was levelling up on him.

'It ain't me you should be huntin' down, Scallon,' he was bawling, 'it's–'

With cold control, Scallon triggered. He couldn't delay his play to hear Hagler out. The owlhoot was too deadly for that and too treacherous. He was making it very clear he did not intend to dangle from a hangman's noose. It was kill or be killed here.

The boom of his Winchester melded with Hagler's barking revolver. Once more violent sound went drumming across the brick and clapboard dwellings of this startled town of Two Pines. Scallon watched Hagler smack back on to the street. A red hole the size of a cent had appeared – stamped into the centre of Hagler's forehead. Brains and other bloody trash were flying out the back of the owlhoot's skull. The mess splattered, mixing with the dust and horse droppings behind him.

Scallon was only vaguely aware of Hagler's lead as it fizzed past him and sprang dust off the boardwalk awning nearby, sending a slat flying crazily upwards before clattering down on to the edge of the walkway.

The woman on the boardwalk shrieked, 'Oh, God in Heaven.'

Scallon still didn't look at her as he jacked in a fresh load but he said, 'I can tell you right now, ma'am, Hagler won't be goin' there. You can lay big odds on that.'

When he did turn to face her he saw she was a pale, petite redhead with big, green eyes. They were staring down at the corpse. With other shocked folk she was standing back against the wall of a large clapboard building that went under the name of Jenny's Eatery. The green gingham gown she wore, with the apron tied over it, fitted tightly against her well-shaped form. Oddly, he found he was faintly stirred by the sight of her female curves, despite the deadly situation that had just passed.

But she was yelling again, 'You've killed him. Cold-bloodedly killed him. He's not the one you should be gunning down.'

'You figure, ma'am?' grunted Scallon tetchily, instantly forgetting his sudden mild interest in her femininity. He scowled across at her. 'Well, I'd contest that,' he rasped peevishly. 'That sonofabitch was out to kill me. He had his gun out. He'd considered his chances. They didn't work out.'

Irritated and now scowling around him,

Scallon became aware of the other members of the public. They were coming out of the hideouts they'd hastily sought while the guns had roared. Scallon saw they were taking turns staring at him, then at the dead Hagler, then back again. He saw awe on some of the faces, open-mouthed shock on others – mean appraisal on other more hardcase members of the audience and he took note of them.

And now, looking beyond them, Scallon could see a burly, thick-set man was hurriedly making his way through the crowd from up-town. When he got near enough Scallon observed he had a round, red face, clear blue eyes and beefy shoulders. A shot-gun was clasped in his right hand. A tin badge was shiny on his grey vest. As he drew close Scallon saw the lawman's blue stare was hard and enquiring as it came off Hagler and rested upon him.

'Well, you'd better start explainin', mister,' he said.

Scallon was happy to see the peace officer

sensibly kept the shot-gun at his side, but he guessed the man would have no qualms about using it if the need arose.

'Be a pleasure,' he said.

TWO

While the lawman had been getting his words out, Scallon was deciphering the engraving on the badge the man toted. It announced the newcomer was a deputy sheriff.

He said, 'I'm Luke Scallon.' He pointed a horny finger at the corpse on the street. 'This here's Ben Hagler. I reckon you must know he's wanted strong in these here parts an' that there's a thousand dollars re-ward been put on his head. Well, I intend to collect that money as soon as is reasonable.'

Before the lawman could reply, the woman's voice interjected again from the boardwalk.

'Luke Scallon, the bounty hunter?' She made it sound as though she was trying to spit something nasty out of her mouth. 'I might have known.'

Glowering, Scallon turned. Normally he wouldn't have bothered to answer – being used to Women's League protestations about his occasional use of crude methods to bring in violent lawbreakers – but there was something about this woman's insistence that was forcing him to reply.

'I give every man his chance,' he snapped. 'You heard me do that, saw me do that.'

The green eyes flashed at him as she tilted her head. 'I did. But I've also heard different about you, Luke Scallon. Dead flesh is money to you. And dead quarry can't speak in its own defence.'

His tetchiness rising like a thunderhead, Scallon took a step forward. 'By God, ma'am, you'd best choose your words with more care from now on.'

Intervening, the lawman moved in front of him. 'Easy,' he said. 'She's jest a little excited.'

Scallon glowered savagely. 'She should button up.'

The lawman nodded, said, 'Sure.' Then he flicked a glance at the woman. 'Go about your business and leave this to me, Jenny. OK?'

The woman cocked her slightly tilted nose into the air. 'Don't get uppity with me, Hank Ruger!' she blazed. She turned and disappeared into the eatery behind her. As she went she was muttering about unbridled shootings and rampant lawlessness on the range and streets.

When she'd gone, the lawman turned to him. Scallon saw Ruger wore a wry but affable smile. The starpacker offered a hand. 'Reckon from that you already got my name,' he said. He now squinted against the sun, his blue gaze neutral. 'And, partly in defence of Jenny, I've also heard a lot about you myself, Scallon. Some good, some bad. But I won't take sides on it.'

Accepting the lawman's offered mitt and shaking it briefly, Scallon then raised dark brows. 'That's somethin', I guess,' he said, though he didn't really give a damn. He could sleep easy with his conscience. But to match Ruger's tentative grin, he allowed what could be passed for a smile to relax the grim, almost bloodless, gash that were his own lips. 'She's a fiesty one,' he admitted. 'Shows spirit. I reckon that's got to be good in this country.'

Ruger nodded. 'And she also serves the best steaks in town,' he said.

Scallon recalled Charlie, the barkeep at John's Place, also endorsing somebody called Jenny Manners' steaks. It was easy to put two and two together, particularly after seeing written in bold black letters JENNY'S EATERY over the door she'd disappeared through.

'So I've been informed,' he said.

Ruger hefted his shot-gun and stared at the sprawled body of Hagler. 'Well, guess that's the last of them,' he said.

Scallon nodded. But he'd never been one for counting heads or making small talk, or discussing what he considered to be finished business. There was now more urgent, *unfinished* business to be dealt with. However, out of courtesy he said, 'Yup, you could say that – the active ones, that is,' before appending, because of his present near-destitute circumstances, 'Now, when can you get authorization through concerning the re-ward?'

Ruger raised brows and pursed thick lips. 'It shouldn't prove to be too difficult,' he said. 'Fact is, Sheriff Boss Falster wired me six days ago about the increased reward placed on Hagler's head and to say that you'd headed out into the mountains after him. Even said you'd probably end up comin' this way and, if that was the case, I should extend every assistance, if needed.'

'That sounds like Falster,' said Scallon. That out he went hip-shot, hooked a thumb into his gunbelt. He was feeling incredibly weary now this grinding month of hard riding was finally over. And with swift precision, he mentally reviewed the circumstances that had brought him here, to the town of Two Pines, just to get the whole business filed away in his mind and done with.

It had started in Rutland, the county seat. Rustling and killing had been rampant on this range. The powers that be had had enough. He'd been hired and deputized to ride with the hastily assembled county posse to help, as Sheriff Boss Falster had put it, give the gathered townsmen some back-bone, they being composed mostly of local businessmen unused to a manhunt and long hours in the saddle. But, as time had gone on, they had proved to be tougher than expected, for it had taken three gruelling weeks to run down Hagler's gang. It was only when they realized the main man, Ben Hagler, wasn't with his boys that they had finally faltered and become disheartened and reckoned they'd done enough.

Scallon raised dark brows. With hindsight, it had been a reasonable reaction. They'd been in desolate country, nary a sign, nor a word, that Hagler was ahead of them. Food stocks had been running low and Sheriff Falster had a leg wound that needed better attention than it had been getting on the trail.

But it was when they had arrived back at Rutland that they'd had to swallow the bitterest pill of all. Hagler, it was announced, while they'd been rampaging around the countryside after his gang, had been holed up on the family's two-bit ranch not ten miles out of town. Nobody had claimed to have known about that fact until the morning the posse returned to town. Then it was announced Hagler had been there all the time and had lit out ahead of them only two hours previously.

Scallon blinked lids over bleak eyes. It was as if, with the collusion of some of his bar cronies, Hagler had been gleefully making mock of their efforts to trap him. For sure, Scallon thought resentfully, it didn't take too much figuring to appreciate Hagler had still got some friends on the range, which had faintly surprised him.

Well, with Falster laid up by his wound and the tired posse of townspeople reluctant to continue because of business commitments, as well as fatigue, the fervour to bring the main lawbreaker to book had diminished. It was considered they'd drawn his sting now they'd killed or captured most of his gang and that he would ride clear of the country for good.

So it hadn't helped Scallon's temper one bit to be aroused from a deep sleep only an hour after he had entered it to be told Falster wanted him urgently. He had reluctantly risen from his hotel bed, dressed and walked grouchily up the street to Falster's neat, picket-fenced, clapboard house on the edge of town.

Staring haggardly up from his sickbed, the county sheriff had said the reward on Hagler had been put up to a thousand dollars and it would be Scallon's if he brought Hagler to swift justice. To help make it official, Falster had added, he could still consider himself deputized.

There was a proviso of a sort, though, Falster went on. The representatives of the Cattlemen's Association and the council would greatly prefer Hagler to be brought in alive, to face a quick trial. Tax-paying folks, the sheriff had dryly informed, appreciated seeing justice done with their own eyes. They liked to pack a picnic, he'd continued, bring the kids into town, make a holiday out of it. Some even took pleasure out of a botched job, Falster included, liked to see a man kick and gag, see his eyes pop, his face swell and go purple as he died slow.

Pushing his thoughts aside for a moment, Scallon stared past Ruger up the broad street of Two Pines and blinked lids over brooding eyes. Cynicism filled him. *And some of the self-righteous sonsofbitches that attended those hangings had the gall to question his own damned methods!*

But, he recalled, it had been at that juncture that he had become curious as to the source of such munificence. He hadn't been surprised when Falster had announced it had been the Wagon Wheel boss, Stimson Randell, who'd put up the other five hundred to make it a round thousand on Hagler's head.

Well, Scallon knew Randell was head of the county's Cattlemen's Association, a leading member of the county council and made no secret of the fact that he intended to run for governor in two years time. Randell was also reputed to be one of the richest and most influential men hereabouts and usually got his own way when he barked loud enough.

On that note Scallon faded his swift review of the events that had finally brought him to Two Pines and the showdown with Ben Hagler.

Answering Ruger he said, 'Guess the sheriff was right in his reckoning about me comin' this way. One thing, though, Ruger: Falster did express a hope I would return Hagler in one piece so they could publicly hang him.' He paused, coughed and rubbed his battered nose before he laid his grey, cold stare on the deputy once more. With a shrug he went on, 'Maybe the council members saw votes in it, or Randell did. I don't know, but I'd appreciate it if you'd explain I had no choice but to do it the way I did and that Hagler'll be buried here because I won't be totin' that sonofabitch back to Rutland, that's fer sure. If it turns out his family want him, they must damn well fetch him.'

'Hagler has more kin?' Ruger looked surprised and narrowed his fleshy eyelids.

Scallon nodded. Gossip around the nightly posse campfires had given him some details, the rest he had found out for himself. 'Yeah. We killed two of his brothers during the hunt for the gang. The youngest one, Elias, lives with his mother on the ranch. His pa's been dead some time. Apparently, Elias's never taken any part in their unlawful activities and has run the spread on his own as best he can. It's said the boy has never held with his brothers' owlhootin' ways.'

'Still could be tricky,' Ruger suggested. 'Blood an' all....'

Scallon raised dark brows. 'Yup, but I hope not.'

Ruger took off his sweat-stained, pearl-grey Stetson and wiped the glistening perspiration off his broad forehead. 'Well, can't see any problem,' he said. 'I'll get the mortician to delay the buryin' a couple of days, give the family time to claim his body.' Then he waved a disparaging arm. 'But, hell, those people down county hall know nothin' about what it's like goin' up against the likes of Hagler – and the pittance they pay their law officers to do so proves that.' Ruger continued to wave an arm, but this time it was conciliatory. 'But I mean no slight on you, Scallon,' he added. He nodded his head vigorously. 'By God, you earned your money here today. An', yeah, I heard you caution that sonofabitch before you fired, saw the way he pulled that other stunt on you. Figure at bottom, everybody'll be glad to hear an end's been put to that no-account, hangin' or no hangin'.'

Thankful and satisfied Ruger was a sensible man, Scallon spat cotton. But to make a slight correction to Ruger's summary, he flipped a rueful glance at Jenny's Eatery. 'Not quite everybody,' he said.

Ruger caught his drift. 'Jenny? Yeah. She can be slightly crazy sometimes. But she shouldn't have any love for Hagler. But I reckon you haven't any interest in the reasons for that right now.'

Scallon raised weary brows. 'No. I ain't. Jest interest in a whole lot of sleep.' He rubbed a grubby hand across his chin-stubble. But, even so, in the calm he now felt, he found he was becoming more and more interested in Stimson Randell, of the vast Wagon Wheel outfit.

Before he'd come up to this country he'd heard of Randell. In fact it had been Stimson Randell who had originally invited him in on top pay to help Boss Falster ginger up the posse he'd been forming to run Hagler to ground. The hiring had happened quick and easy. He'd brought a wanted bank thief and killer into Rutland to claim the reward on him. Randell had been in town and had sent for him.

Scallon raised dark brows. Fact was, Stimson Randell had given him the impression he had an almost unhealthy ambition to have Hagler rubbed out, though he, Scallon, hadn't voiced that opinion outright. He was a businessman. He'd been invited to do a job and he would do it. He wasn't concerned about other shenanigans on the range. But even Boss Falster had expressed that he was more than a little puzzled by Randell's seemingly consuming urge to bring Hagler to heel. Trouble had been on the boil on the range for some time and Stimson was the one who had been losing cattle heavily and had a right to feel aggrieved.

Scallon squinted up the now busy main street once more. But coming right down to it, who knew what motivated men? And why? Particularly ambitious, powerful men like Randell. Again, to be cynical, maybe the rancher simply saw votes in his obsession to get Hagler ... or any owlhoot plaguing the range. Even so, Scallon mused, Randell had come over as an arrogant, ruthless, cigar-chewing bastard who thought he could buy anybody, or anything.

Scallon stuck out his jaw. But to hell with that. His business was hunting down men for the price on their heads, not the politics behind it, and that was what he had done for Randell and the county. And because of that, a few hours from now, he would be a thousand dollars richer and heading for new pastures.

'You recommend a hotel?' he said to Ruger.

The deputy pursed his lips again, looked a little dubious about giving the recommendation he appeared to have in mind. 'Not a *hotel* exactly,' he said tentatively. 'Jenny Manners agin. She also owns a large rooming house, takes in boarders. Truth be known, you won't find a better outfit anywhere for price and cleanliness.'

Scallon raised dark brows at the news. 'Hell, that woman seems to pop up everywhere.'

Ruger grinned broadly. 'Jenny's just a very busy li'l lady. A little crazy sometimes, like I say, but out to make a million, is my guess.'

Though not entirely happy with the information, Scallon nodded briskly at Ruger. 'Well, my thanks, deputy.'

Now he squinted against the sun, which was slightly over its zenith and beginning to wester and make small shadows on Two Pines' broad main street. There was still the pressing matter of the reward. Things weren't entirely settled between him and Ruger concerning that. And after the disastrous accident he'd had in the mountains, Scallon decided ready money was a matter of urgent concern to him.

'I can expect to hear from you purty soon?' he ventured.

For a moment Ruger blankly looked at him.

Scallon prompted, 'The re-ward money?'

Ruger swiftly raised enlightened brows. 'Oh, yeah. Well, from what I've heard, there'll be no problem there. Soon as I have clearance from Rutland an' got it from the bank, it'll be in your hand.'

Scallon felt satisfaction fill him, but said, 'Well, I ain't in *that* big a rush, Ruger. Tomorrow mornin'll do. Right now, I got a mess of sleep to catch up on.'

Ruger nodded, flicked a quick glance over the tall bounty hunter's haggard, battered features. 'Fair enough.' Then he narrowed his eyelids. 'You thinkin' of stayin' on after collectin'?'

Scallon shook his head. 'Naw. Shouldn't think so. Things seem pretty well played out around here.'

Though Ruger looked slightly relieved by that, he said, 'I guess that's usual, bein' in your line of business.' He raised sandy eyebrows. 'Got a few dodgers in the office you might be interested in....'

Scallon wiped a hand across his drawn, dirty face and drew himself up. That was a nice gesture. 'My thanks, Ruger. Maybe some could prove useful. Now, if you don't mind, like I said, I got a little sleep to catch up on.'

Ruger nodded understandingly. 'Sure ... an' about the reward: should have things sewn up real good by morning.' He stared down at Hagler's dead body. 'Now, guess I'd better see to the corpse an' get that hoss of his rounded up.'

Scallon nodded. However, he found there was still one more thing rankling him, for he had this probing, curious mind that liked to know the facts, tie up loose ends. 'Just one last point, Ruger: seein' as how you didn't know Hagler had kin ... you been in these parts long yourself?'

The lawman grinned. He even looked pleased. 'Well, you sure fit your reputation for thoroughness. Two months. Buzz Graham, sheriff over at Bleater County ...

you know him?'

Scallon nodded.

'Well, he recommended me to Boss Falster. Because of the troubles on this range, Boss had been looking for reinforcements and wired Graham. My job over there was on the line anyway, with Bleater County in the throes of slimming down its police force in a drive for economy and I felt like a change. Falster accepted Graham's recommendation, so here I am.'

Scallon rubbed the side of his scarred face with a large hand. He was beginning to like the way Ruger looked at things. 'Jest wondered, Hank,' he said, 'jest wondered. Be seein' you.'

He headed up the street, his empty belly the next priority.

THREE

Having stalled the big roan at the large livery stables north of town and given brisk instructions as to how he wanted the horse treated – good grooming, good grain and clean straw bedding – Scallon now stood inside Jenny's Eatery, staring over the till counter by the door into Miss Manners' startled green eyes.

'You!' she said.

'Yup. Me agin, ma'am,' he said.

The tautness that had kept him wound up this past month was relaxed even more now and he attempted to put a slight hint of amusement into his deep-set, brooding eyes. He did find the situation between himself and the woman a little ridiculous and felt a need to improve it.

'I'd like some food, a bath and a bed, in

that order, ma'am,' he went on. 'You've come highly recommended to supply all those needs.'

Still looking slightly startled she said, 'I have?'

Scallon grinned, but knew it was more of a grimace.

'You have,' he said.

Around him, Scallon could hear that the clatter of men eating off real china plates using real fancy bone-handled knives and forks had lifted again. It had gone a mite quiet when he had first walked in.

Jenny Manners said, 'Well, I must say, you've got gall coming in here after what passed between us out there just now.' He saw the challenge had come back to her eyes.

Seeing it, Scallon sighed tiredly. He pushed back his battered brown hat with a thumb and rubbed his hollow eyes. He didn't know why he wanted to continue to try and mollify this woman, but he did. He stared at her for a moment before he

41

quietened himself again. 'Ma'am,' he said patiently, his voice rasping harshly with the fatigue in him, 'Hagler was a no-good sonofabitch and deserved the fate he got. If you've been in the territory long enough, you ought to know that.'

Jenny Manners tilted her chin defiantly, but she looked a little flattened by his words. 'I've been around long enough,' she said. 'Agreeing's another thing.' She paused, eyeing him. It seemed, at last, she was giving the matter some consideration. She sighed. 'Well, I guess, in the end you had little choice but do what you did.' She paused again, as if doing some more inner debating, then said, 'A room with meals is two dollars a day. The bath I'll throw in if you're stopping more than three days.'

Oddly, Scallon found he was relieved by the woman's turn-around. Usually, he'd have just gone elsewhere and to hell with her, if her hostility had continued. 'Guess I'll have to pay for the bath,' he said. 'Hope to be ridin' on tomorrow.'

Jenny Manners didn't appear concerned by that. 'In that case it'll be an extra dollar. But you get soap, hot water and a big clean towel.'

At that, Scallon's natural-born carefulness where money was concerned now welled up in him, despite his fatigue. 'Damn it. A dollar? Just for a bath?'

Jenny Manners raised her shapely brows, as if slightly taken aback by his enquiry, but instantly contemptuous of his attempt to modify the deal. 'You can use the creek, if you don't like the prices,' she snapped. She wrinkled her snub nose. 'You smell as though you need to do something about your condition pretty quick.'

Scallon ignored her scathing comment, shuffled and stared irately. 'Damn it, you drive a hard bargain, ma'am, that's all I can say,' he snorted petulantly. 'I figure fifty cents to be plenty fer a bath.'

She tilted her chin again. 'Randell's Hotel – Stimson Randell's place up the road a-piece – charges two dollars. Up there they're not averse to using the same water twice. You can take it from me, Mr Scallon, my prices are the keenest in town.'

Just then a trail-dusted rider came in, spurs jingling. It disrupted Scallon's surprise at learning Randell owned a hotel in town. But, it shouldn't have, he decided. Randell was a go-ahead – as was Jenny Manners, it seemed.

The puncher paused at the till counter, pushed his hat up on to the top of his forehead. He grinned broadly. 'Howdy, Miz Jenny. Usual, if you please. All the trimmings.'

Jenny Manners' gaze slid to the cowboy for a moment. She said, 'Coming right up, Joe.' She turned towards a door which clearly led to the kitchen, judging by the steam. 'Jane ... steak rare with trimmings, for Joe Drennen.'

As the cowboy bow-legged off to find a seat, Scallon met Miss Manners' enquiring stare as it came impatiently back to him. 'You made up your mind yet, mister?'

He sighed. He'd give it one more try. 'Ain't you even prepared to negotiate?'

'No, and it's cash in advance,' said Jenny Manners firmly.

Scallon winced at this further blow. Cash in advance? Now, that was the last thing he wanted to hear. He didn't have a cent to his name. He'd spent what loose change he'd had on the beer and livery charges. Fact was, his money belt, with all the wealth he'd had in the world stashed in it (three thousand dollars), was gone. He still couldn't believe the stitching on the belt buckle had parted while he'd swam, hanging on to the roan, across that swift-flowing mountain river back there when in the pursuit of Ben Hagler. Now, it felt hellishly uncomfortable to be a temporary pauper.

'Damn it, ma'am,' he murmured, 'can't it wait?' His embarrassment caused heat to come to his lean, battered face. He bent closer. He whispered, 'Fact is, I can't pay right now.' He paused to try and come to terms with his unfamiliar feelings of chagrin. 'I got the re-ward money comin' through any time. If you ain't sure I'm good for it, ask Deputy Ruger. He'll vouch for me.'

Scallon realized the talk around him had lowered again, to catch what he was saying, but his scowl around the room lifted it again, rapidly.

When he returned his gaze he saw Miss Manners was staring at him, as if appraising his disreputable appearance. Then he heard her sigh.

'You look all in,' she said at length, as though she'd found some sympathy for him at last, even if she gave the impression she felt she was going against her better judgement by admitting it. She pursed her pretty lips. 'OK, I'll risk it.' She paused for a moment before she added, 'And if you've got a change of clothes, I'll also see those you have on are sent up to the Chinaman for cleaning and repair. He's cheap, but good. Your bath I'll have prepared while you eat.'

Relieved that at last the woman appeared to be showing some charity, Scallon felt the slight tension, brought on by his financial embarrassment, fall away. It seemed, at bottom, like most women, Jenny Manners had her soft centre. He was mighty grateful for that.

'You won't regret this, ma'am,' he said. 'You'll find Luke Scallon's never welched on a debt in his life.' Scallon found her green gaze was sceptical as it held on him.

'Is that so?' she said. 'Well, time will tell, I guess.'

FOUR

Scallon struggled through the veils of sleep that were still insisting he should continue with his slumber. His drowsy thoughts were emphatic: to hell with the constant hammering on the bedroom door. The single iron-frame bed he lay on, the sheets and blankets he was wrapped in, were far too comfortable. But the knocking continued, relentlessly.

'Yeah?' he finally growled. He found his throat, once more, was as dry as the Sonora desert. 'This had better be good,' he warned.

'Hank Ruger, Scallon.'

'Then what?'

'Got some news you maybe won't like.'

'I'll be the judge of that.'

'Stimson Randell wants you to ride on

over to the Wagon Wheel, collect the reward money there,' Ruger drawled. 'Wired the reason was he has more work for you.'

Scallon reared up on one elbow and glared at the door. 'He what? Damnation. I got debts to cover here before I can go anywhere,' he rasped.

Ruger cleared his throat. 'Yeah,' he said. 'Jenny Manners has already mentioned that to me. I explained it to Randell. Randell said he'd take care of it. He has.'

Scallon felt anger flicker through him. 'Well, hell, he's got a damned gall,' he growled. 'I take care of my own business.'

He burrowed into the pillows again, wanting to finish his sleep, but found it had become harder to accomplish because of the news Ruger had brought. Just what had Randell got in mind? However, he felt the issue did not give him a strong enough incentive, yet, to discontinue his sleep.

He growled, 'Well, OK, you've told me, Hank. My thanks. Don't make too much noise leavin' the buildin'.'

There was a moment's silence before Ruger persisted, 'Randell wired it was urgent. Gave the impression he needed you to get down to the Wagon Wheel, rightaway.'

Once more Scallon reared his head off the pillow, his anger filling out. 'For Christ's sake, what's so damned urgent?' he said.

'He didn't say in the wire,' Ruger said. 'Guess he reckons when he shouts, everybody jest naturally has to jump.'

Scallon rumbled sourly, 'You figure, huh? Well, I ain't *everybody*.'

Nevertheless, Scallon swung his legs off the bed and placed his bare feet on to the floor and sat rubbing his sleep-fattened face. In the end, business was business.

'Time is it, Ruger?' he said.

Beyond the thin door, Ruger sniffed. 'Ten in the mornin'. Thursday, that is. You've been asleep damn near two days, Scallon.'

Luke was jolted rudely wide awake by that. Two days? But, yes, during the dark hours, he did vaguely remember using the john out the back of the rooming house a couple of times, then gulping a draught of water from the jug on the washstand when he'd returned, before the oblivion of sleep had swiftly overtaken him again.

Damn it, he'd hoped to be back on the trail yesterday and, by now, far away from here. He hustled to his feet.

'Ruger, I need money right away,' he rasped.

As the drugging effect of his long sleep dispersed and he became fully cognizant, Scallon realized he was becoming ever more exasperated with the situation he had awakened to. And not helping his bad humour, the strong rays of the sun, filtering in through a gap in the curtains up to the small window, were hitting him right in the eyes, causing him to raise his hand and wrinkle his gaze against their harsh glare.

Ruger was saying, 'Randell anticipated that. Wired giving me authorization to draw fifty dollars out of his account at the Two Pines bank – he owns it – and hand it to you to pay for trail provisions an' whatever else you might need.'

Though Scallon found the news salved his grumpiness a little, he growled, 'God damn, to hell with him. He seems to take a lot fer granted.'

He scrubbed his two-day stubble and calmed himself. No use taking it out on the lawman. 'Well, jest give me twenty minutes, Hank, to get my horse an' possibles.'

'Will do,' said the lawman.

Scallon listened to the noise of Ruger's boots hitting the boards of the landing until it was lost amongst the noise of traffic on the street coming in through the slightly open window of his bedroom. As he dressed Scallon was surprised to find his gear had been crisply laundered and laid out ... Jenny Manners and the Chinaman?

Half an hour later Scallon picked up the silver dollars lying on the lawman's office desk and put them in the doeskin bag he carried especially for that purpose. He slipped it into his vest pocket, then ventured a smile in Ruger's direction.

'Right to the last cent,' he said.

'Need your signature,' the lawman said, indicating with his stubby index finger to the ruled book on the desk before him.

Scallon raised dark brows. 'Sure.' He picked up the pen beside the book and dipped it into the inkwell, which was sunk into the scarred desk. He wrote his name with firm, flourishing authority, dotting the end of the signature and underlining it.

He put down the pen and raised keen eyes. 'You mentioned folders the other day....' he said.

Ruger arched his sandy brows. He fumbled in the drawer set in the right side of the desk he was sat at. He brought up six sheets. Scallon searched them with a professional eye, shuffling quickly through them.

'Three could be useful,' he said. He folded the dodgers and pocketed them. 'My thanks, Ruger.'

'You considered any other line of work?' Ruger said casually. He played with the pencil in his hand, his gaze only half-interested.

'Time or two.' Scallon rubbed his chin. He found Ruger easy to talk to, and now and again he did have this urge to open out a little to some people, especially when he was feeling good. 'One time – when I got shot up real bad. Another time, when I was forced to shoot a woman.'

Ruger showed interest in that. He said, 'Somehow, that don't seem to fit the hard but fair reputation of Luke Scallon.'

'Thank you, an' it don't,' Scallon admitted. 'I pleaded with her not to push it. When she brought it to a showdown, it was the closest I ever got to bein' out-drawn an' lyin' dead. She was slicker with a Colt than any hardcase I've ever run up against. That lady was a real bitch-of-a-bitch.'

'Still, I guess havin' to do that kind of thing don't sit well with you,' Ruger said, 'even if you had no choice. Am I right?'

'You are,' admitted Scallon. 'But I can't speak for everybody. Some varmints I know wouldn't think twice about shootin' down a woman, if it'd further their ends.'

'I guess so,' Ruger said.

Smiling, he rose and leaned across the desk. Scallon took his firm grip once more, shook it briskly.

'Well, luck, Scallon,' the deputy said.

Scallon nodded. 'An' you, Ruger.' He meant it. He tapped the folders in his pocket. 'Figure I'll send you ten per cent of the re-wards on these, if I run them to ground.'

Ruger stared, surprised. 'Though I ain't complainin', that wasn't the motive behind handing them over,' he said.

'I know that, Hank,' Scallon said. He touched the brim of his hat with a long finger. 'Hope to see more of you, sometime.'

Out on the street he approached his big roan, tied to the rail before the lawman's office. The livery stable had taken good care of the beast. As promised, he rode back to clear the extra day's stabling he owed for and to give the hostler an extra buck for his expert ministrations.

Then he swung up again, clicked at the mare and dug his heels in gently. Three hundred yards up the busy, dry, wheel-rutted street – outside Jenny's Eatery – he climbed down and tied the horse to the long rail fronting it.

Inside, even at half-past ten in the morning, he found the place busy. Jenny Manners was again sitting at the till counter, just inside the door.

He touched his battered hat. 'Ma'am,' he said. 'I could use some breakfast. Heard my account's been taken care of.'

Jenny Manners, all business, nodded. She said, 'It has.' As her green-eyed perusal latched on to him, Scallon reckoned it missed little of his scarred, now clean-shaven, tough-looking face and she met his returned gaze unflinchingly. 'I owe you two dinners and two breakfasts,' she went on, after moments. She added with a touch of irony, 'You sleep long and heavy, Mr Scallon. I even had a man look in on you one time, to return your laundry and to see if you were still alive.'

'I hope you weren't too disappointed when he found I was,' he quipped. 'And thanks for seein' my washing got done.'

Her green stare was raking and looked angry when it came flashing back at him. 'Part of the service and paid for. Regarding maybe finding you dead, it might surprise you to learn, Mr Scallon, I was concerned. You're not being funny.'

Scallon decided he had hit slightly below the belt. 'No, ma'am,' he said. 'I guess not. Ham and eggs'll be fine.'

'Double ham and eggs,' Jenny Manners bellowed to the kitchen. Then her gaze engaged his again. 'That do?'

'Generous, ma'am.'

Scallon grinned at her, but he knew it would look more like a grimace. For twenty-three years he'd never been able to smile normally. Since being a boy of eight he'd had this stiffness in the right side of his face, ever since he had been punched near silly by the school bully. The sonofabitch had been two years older than him.

Scallon recalled his pa had wanted to step in, see the bully's parents, but he'd pleaded with him not to. Instead, he'd vowed never to let that kind of thing happen to him again. He had immediately and secretly enlisted the help of a black-sheep uncle, who'd had a homestead by Valley Creek a mile out of the town he was born in and who, at one time, had been a successful bare-fist fighter as well as hell-raiser.

With Uncle Wilfrid's guidance, plus his own fanatical zeal, he had practised the arts of pugilism – along with a mess of barroom tricks also known to his uncle, but not to be found in any textbooks. Three months later, toughened up and filled out, he'd called the no good sonofabitch bully out and battered him senseless right there on Main Street, for all to see. He'd lived a trouble-free childhood after that.

Scallon made for a table near the street window and sat down. It was a thing he wouldn't normally do – expose himself like this – but he was feeling good and he felt sure there was no danger to him on this range … not any more.

There was a tablecloth on which were laid bone-handled knives and forks and a clean serviette. He raised dark brows. Well, for sure, Jenny Manners did things in style. He relaxed, his rumbling stomach – made lean through lack of food because of his long sleep – anticipating the meal to come.

He was rolling a quirly when the window shattered, showering him with glass. The roar of the rifle accompanying the noise savaged the amiable quiet of the eating-room. The slug of lead from it splintered the table an inch from Scallon's stomach and he went to ground, dragging out his Colt as he did so.

With anger surging through him, he bellied forward and peered over the low timber front that had supported the splintered window. As his hard gaze searched the street – which was quickly emptying of wagons, horses and people – more lead came, but it was aimed high, and that puzzled him. Nevertheless, he crouched behind the low frame he'd landed against. Behind him, yelps were coming from the diners around as they pressed their bodies to the floor.

Scallon's keen gaze soon found the puffs of gunsmoke coming from the alley across the street. The bushwhacker, he could see, was behind a pile of boxes on an elevated goods platform over there.

Scallon triggered his Colt, though he knew he had little hope of doing much damage with it. The range was too great and his rifle – which would have had the range – was in its saddle scabbard.

In reply to his shots, lead raked the flimsy cover he crouched behind. He felt a sting of pain in his thigh. Then, to his left, a rifle opened up. He saw lead rip chunks of wood out of the boxes the bushwhacker was sheltering behind. Scallon's surprised, sidelong glance told him Jenny Manners was firing the Winchester that was helping him, while standing in plain view at the open doorway.

'For God's sake, get into cover, ma'am,' he bawled anxiously.

In response, Jenny Manners crouched down, jacked off three more shots in professional style. The lead battered the ambusher's cover, one piece of shot ricocheting off into the bald, cobalt sky with a snarling whine.

Two more hasty shots came from the bushwhacker, then it went quiet. Only the metallic sound of Jenny Manners jacking another load into her Winchester broke the shocked silence. A swift glance to his right told Scallon Jenny was peering forward expectantly, as if, this time, waiting for a tangible target.

Moments later the ambusher broke cover, surging out – astride a big, light bay horse – from behind the piled boxes on the raised platform that had screened him. His face was masked by his bandanna. But, thought

Scallon meanly, the bay horse he would remember, and the man's buckskin coat. The whole incident, he realized, hadn't lasted a minute.

Jenny's Winchester cracked twice, but her lead failed to find the quickly moving target.

For moments, the breathless silence that descended after the roar of guns, once more was total, then the buzz of talk rose as people began to cautiously come out from cover.

Scallon noticed, as he straightened from his flimsy shelter and held his damaged thigh, that the stares that came his way were fierce and hostile and the knots of towns-people gathered on the street began gesturing in his direction. He recognized quickly, at this particular moment, that he was not a popular man in Two Pines. He thought it very doubtful if he ever had been.

'Anybody know him?' he demanded.

'Too busy bitin' dust to see a damned thing,' said one.

Somebody behind Scallon growled, 'God

damn it, mister, it'll be a good day fer this town when you've gone.'

He turned to see a glaring, irate cowman standing nearby. His scattered meal was on the floor and half of it on his vest where he had fallen on it when he had hurriedly hit the boards. Scallon could also see more angry stares were coming his way from other diners who had taken similar precautions.

He snorted indignantly. 'Me? Why not blame that sonofabitch out there?' he roared.

'No way,' rumbled another of the diners. 'It's the damned trade you're in. You draw lead like honey draws bear. You ain't no right to move among decent folk like this, puttin' them in danger.'

Scallon glared around him while reloading his Colt. 'Well, to hell with you,' he shouted.

He shook out empty shell cases. With the sixshooter armed with five bullets once more, hammer resting on the empty chamber, he strode towards the door.

He could see Jenny Manners was calmly propping her Winchester against the pay desk. He stopped by her side. 'Ma'am,' he said briskly, while glowering around him, 'to be sure, right now, you'd make more man than any two of these sonsofbitches. I mightily thank you fer what you did just now.'

Looking serenely calm Jenny said, 'You're wounded, Mr Scallon.'

Surprised by such composure, he said, 'Well, I thank you for your concern, ma'am, but it's jest a scratch an' nothing to heed. Thing is' – he waved an arm in the general direction the bushwhacker had taken – 'I have to get after that sonofabitch.'

Jenny Manners' green, cool stare still held his own. It was still unperturbed. 'My guess is he will head for the mess of badlands three miles on from where he hit the range when he left town. That tangle of rock makes for difficult tracking. I know. I chased a bunch of rustlers into there five months back. I soon came to realize I was wasting my time, and the time of my six hands.'

'I've tracked through bad country before,' Scallon rumbled impatiently. He didn't like his decisions, or his abilities, questioned.

Jenny Manners' green gaze was still calm. 'I'm sure you have.' She shrugged in her blue gingham, as if to express her indifference. 'OK, Mr Scallon. Have it your way. It's no skin off my hide.'

Scallon paused in his reply. Did she say *my six hands* just now? Surprised anew he asked, 'You got a spread, ma'am?'

She nodded. 'I own the Circle M, up Pershay Canyon. I run a thousand head.'

'Well, damn me.' Scallon stared, openly admiring this tough, petite redhead. 'I gotta say, you is one very busy lady.'

'I'm being rustled, too,' she said, the touch of irony in her voice plain.

That surprised him more and it prompted the question, 'So why ball me out fer killin' Hagler? Seems I've done you a favour.'

She raised shapely brows. 'That's a matter of opinion. Even with Hagler's death, the troubles on this range aren't over.'

Scallon narrowed his eyelids. Was she suggesting there were more rustlers? Was that the reason Stimson Randell wanted him down at the Wagon Wheel?

'How d'you know?' he said.

Her green stare was direct. 'I know. Call it gut-instinct, if you like.'

Scallon 'harrumped'. 'That don't go to provin' much, ma'am,' he said.

'Who do you reckon was doing the shooting just now?' she said.

Scallon shrugged and squinted. 'I don't know. But in my trade you do make enemies, Miss Manners.'

'You're supposed to have ridded this range of its troubles,' she said, 'and along with it any enemies it may have produced to trouble you.'

The swift retort surprised him and she had a fancy way with words. 'Yeah, must admit it does kind of put that theory in doubt, though Hagler still has family.'

Just then Hank Ruger came in through the

door, shot-gun in hand. His blue stare was enquiring as Scallon met it.

'OK, what is it this time?' he demanded. 'God damn, trouble jest seems to follow you around.'

'Bushwhacker,' Scallon said.

Ruger's eyes rounded. 'After you?'

'Seems that way.'

'Why?'

Scallon stared. 'Hell, I'm in a dangerous business.'

Ruger narrowed lids over keen blue eyes. 'What you aim to do about it?'

Scallon scowled. It didn't even need thinking about. 'Head out after the sonofabitch,' he said, 'what d'you think?'

The lawman hefted his shot-gun. 'In that case, I figure to ride with you.'

Scallon shook his head reluctantly, but firmly. 'Well, don't get the notion I ain't grateful for the offer, Hank. However, it's my business. I'll settle it my way.'

'I reckon Boss Falster would like the sonofabitch brought in whole,' ventured

Ruger. 'There's too many things happenin' on this range that don't fit. Questions need to be asked of people who may have answers.'

Scallon stared at the blocky lawman. 'Meanin' he won't be brought in whole if I light out after him alone?'

Ruger's gaze was cool and level. 'You have that reputation.'

Scallon found he wasn't offended, for, more often than not, it usually did work out that way. 'I'll see what I can do about keepin' his hide intact,' he said. 'Fact is, I've got a few questions I'd like to put to that nasty piece of work myself.' He turned to Jenny Manners. 'You think ten dollars will cover the damage done to the window, ma'am?' he said.

He met her green gaze as it swung to meet his own. It was long and searching before she said, 'That could have been nothing to do with you, Mr Scallon. Perhaps you just happened to be there. Maybe somebody is warning me.'

Scallon stared. '*You...?*'

Jenny Manners' bold green gaze was now direct, almost defiant. 'A while ago I helped some people settle on the south range.'

'You *what?*' Scallon's stare became more keen. 'Now, in cattle country, that really would stir up trouble,' he felt inclined to add. 'Again ... why? You're a rancher. Ain't you supposed to hate squatters' guts?'

Jenny Manners' chin lifted more, almost arrogantly. 'The matter was simple enough,' she said. 'First, they weren't squatters. I discovered they had legal title. They're ex-soldiers with their families, given land grants for services to their country. Faced with that, I felt it was the least I could do.'

Scallon nodded. 'Well, I've heard about that kind of thing bein' done,' he said. 'But it won't sit well with the likes of Stimson Randell. Ain't he been runnin' cattle on that range?'

Jenny Manners' pretty face stiffened. 'Yes, he has and is still trying to, but if he is such a pillar of law and order as he claims to be on this range, it'll *have* to sit well with him, as you put it. He will have to accept he no longer has any title to that land, if he ever did have.'

Surprising Scallon, Jenny put a scathing bite into her words. It prompted a quick, questing reply from him. 'He been hurrahin' the settlers?' he said.

Jenny Manners raised her attractive brows. 'He's ruthless enough.'

Scallon stared. 'You ain't answered my question.'

Hank Ruger cut in, shaking his head vigorously and growling, 'Now hold on, Jenny. You can't go around sayin' such things.'

Jenny's eyes were wide. 'What have I said?'

Ruger looked disgruntled. 'Nothin' definite, I guess. But you've been makin' an awful lot of dubious suggestions lately. Stimson Randell has every reason to be riled up about what's happened, but he'll handle it legally.'

Scallon cleared his throat, shuffled, when

he realized he could be getting tangled up in range politics. Hell, what did the troubles on this section of country matter to him, apart from the business angle? Though he found he was intrigued by the revelations he'd been exposed to, there were more pressing matters on his agenda. Like the sonsofbitch riding hell-for-leather away from here and reward money awaiting him at the Wagon Wheel.

'Well, it ain't my business right now,' he said, 'an' this discussion ain't doin' a damn thing to catch that gun-crazy bastard.'

Jenny Manners sighed. 'Very well, if you insist on going, at least let me give you your breakfast and doctor your leg before you set out on your wild-goose chase.'

Stung, Scallon glowered. 'Wild goose chase?' He straightened. 'Sometimes, ma'am,' he rumbled, 'you have a cutting way of putting things. I'll have you know I've successfully tracked hardcases through some of the roughest country known to man.'

Jenny Manners didn't bat an eyelid. 'Even so, I know that particular piece of country you'll be headed for.'

'Well, damn it, you could just be in for a surprise,' snorted Scallon.

To emphasize his point he jerked up straight. For his grumpiness, he was rewarded with pain spearing into his thigh. Clearly, the initial numbness had worn off. He gasped as nausea washed through him. When it had cleared he grunted, 'Well, on second thoughts, maybe I will take you up on your offer to feed an' doctor me first.'

Now Ruger gestured with the hand that held the shot-gun. 'If Jenny's right in thinking it's the badlands he's headed for, she could be right about losin' him. It's one hell of a place. You need company?'

Scallon found the pain of his leg was now making him feel even more irritable. However, he didn't allow it to impinge on their conversation.

'Well, don't get me wrong, Hank,' he said. 'I'm grateful for your offer. But I'm used to working alone, an' old habits die hard. However, there's one thing you could do – let Stimson Randell know it may be some time before I get to the Wagon Wheel.'

'You still working for him?' Jenny Manners cut in crisply. As well as surprise, there was slight contempt in her tone.

It sent another niggle of anger scurrying through Scallon. 'He and the county council owes me near a thousand dollars for nailin' Hagler's hide,' he rumbled. 'I aim to collect. What I do after that'll be my business, Miss Manners.'

Jenny Manners' emerald gaze flashed fire for a moment. 'Will it?' she rapped, then she quickly hid her clear dislike for his answer. She sighed. 'Well, you'd better come through to the back if you want your leg fix–'

The stark, feminine scream cutting off Jenny's words startled Scallon. A door, set in the far wall of the eatery, now banged open and a coloured woman came running in, waving her arms frantically in the air. 'De

Lawd have mercy on us, Miss Jenny,' she was wailing. 'It's Jimmy Blue. He's cold stone daid.'

For a moment Jenny Manners stared blankly at the agitated Negress. 'Jimmy Blue?' she breathed. 'Where, Jane, where?'

Jane waved an anxious arm. 'Back o' dat sto'-room door, Miz Jenny. Shot right through de haid, he is. Po' Jimmy Blue.'

Erupting into motion, Jenny Manners paced to the door Jane had come out of. Scallon, right behind her, noticed two bullet holes were scarring the thin panels, head high.

Right in what Scallon recognized was the line of fire of the bushwhacker lay sprawled a grey-haired, scrawny individual. Blood covered his face and the floorboards around his still body.

'Who is he?' Scallon said.

'The town drunk,' provided a bleak-eyed Ruger, who was right behind him. 'Jenny hires him to keep the place clean, do some liftin' for her.'

Scallon stared at the now clearly shocked and white-faced Miss Manners. 'Correct, ma'am?'

She nodded and turned, putting her hands to her face. For moments she was still, as if thinking, pulling herself together. When she turned her eyes on to him again they had the appearance of orbs of the hardest emerald.

'This makes what I believe was an attempt to hurrah me, now murder,' she said. 'Jimmy never hurt a fly in his life, never carried a gun.'

Scallon caught Ruger's stare. The lawman said, 'An' I guess this puts the decision beyond doubt as to who goes on this ride. It's a matter for the law.' He narrowed his gaze. 'But I could use help. You still deputized?'

Scallon nodded. Boss Falster had asked him to raise his hand a month ago. Nothing had happened since then to rescind it. 'I guess so,' he said.

'Then that settles it.'

Scallon stared at the calm lawman. 'Reckon it does.' His leg was now throbbing savagely. He looked at Jenny Manners. 'But first, it would help to get my leg fixed.... Ma'am, is the offer still open?'

Already, Scallon observed, Jenny Manners seemed to be herself again – cool and self-assured. 'It's still open, Mr Scallon,' she said.

She turned to the coloured woman who was still agitated and shaking. 'Jane, get some hot water and bandages,' she ordered.

Clearly wanting to be out of this room of death Jane said, 'Yes'm. Right away. But what about po' Jimmy Blue?'

All around, the occupants of the eatery were now recovered and buzzing with talk and clearly very shocked. Jenny Manners glared and said, 'Well, who's going to take the body down to that barber who calls himself a mortician?'

Two men volunteered, then Miss Manners turned and said, 'Come with me, Mr Scallon.' But before she moved she glanced sharply at the deputy. 'Can't you disperse these people, Hank?' she demanded abruptly. 'I'm closing for the day.'

Scallon allowed himself a surge of respect. There was no hedging where Jenny Manners was concerned. She was pure steel.

FIVE

Scallon, with Hank Ruger at his side and grim purpose in both of them – the promised large breakfast comfortably under his belt and his leg adequately doctored by Jenny Manners – left the browned range around the town and entered the sprawling, rocky badlands ahead of them. On the outskirts of town he and Ruger soon picked up the bushwhacker's tracks and, as Jenny Manners had predicted, it had led them into those barren, stony hills. As they negotiated the huge sprawl of shale and boulders his original feelings of optimism gradually degenerated into doubt until he halted them. He glanced at Ruger. 'See what she means,' he said, scowling around him. 'This could take a long time.'

The lawman nodded, his face grim. 'One

hell of a place,' he acknowledged.

Both men settled into saddles, their eyes patiently searching for tracks. Noon passed, blisteringly hot. By now, the search had become dogged. They'd barely covered six miles in three hours, but, Scallon thankfully observed now, the dense crowd of huge rocks they had been painstakingly working their way through were, at last, beginning to tail out. Soon open country, spread below rising benches of soil-thin strata which curved in huge sweeps into the hazy distance to the west, was making decipher-ing the trail a little easier.

Scallon set his jaw into a firm line. A measure of satisfaction settled in him. For sure, judging by the clearer tracks they were now encountering, maybe the sonofabitch ahead was figuring he'd done enough to escape them in those rocks back there. Well, perhaps where most trackers were con-cerned, that could well have been the case. Scallon blinked lids over bleak eyes. But not where Luke Scallon was concerned.

However, though the country they were passing through was now easier, he and Ruger still frequently lost the tracks the killer had left. They continually had to quarter the ground to pick it up again.

Twenty miles on and an hour from sunset, Ruger reined in, pulled out a handkerchief, mopped his streaming brow and took a long drink from his canteen. As he did, he stared at the ranks of firs now spiking the higher ground two miles ahead of their position, then he glanced at the big and, at the moment, taciturn manhunter on the roan beside him.

'Hell, you sure push a man, Luke,' he complained. 'You ever give up?'

Though his thigh was throbbing fit to bust, Scallon shook his head. 'No, I don't. And you gotta let men know that.' He stared evenly at the lawman. 'Hank, you can go back if you don't feel up to it. I won't think the worse of you.'

Ruger scowled, clearly resentful. His round face reddened even more. 'To hell with that,' he growled. 'I'll match you – step for step, all the way. Bet on it.'

Scallon shaped his bleak, deformed smile. 'Though I kind of anticipated that answer,' he said, 'I'm sure glad to hear it from the horse's mouth, pardner.'

Now he let his narrow gaze take in the treeline ahead. There were places there which were built for ambush. And the faint tracks the bushwhacker had left were heading straight for them. But he had a sneaking feeling their quarry was maybe thinking he'd given them the slip, or was maybe assuming no pursuit had been made in the first place and had relaxed from the start, not knowing he'd killed a man. Scallon licked his dry lips. On the other hand....

'I figure that sonofabitch could have looked back, seen us, and is maybe up there waitin' fer us,' Ruger said, breaking in on Scallon's train of thought.

Scallon was taken by surprise. It was as though the lawman had snatched away the very conclusions he himself was coming to.

He rubbed a hand down his gaunt cheek. It rasped on the bristles and came away damp with sweat. 'Well, I'm with you on that, Hank. So I figure we should split up; go at him from two directions. Get him in two minds, if he *is* layin' fer us.'

Ruger nodded soberly. 'My figurin', too.'

Again, Scallon scanned the ground ahead. He could see there was a low ridge to the west, overlooking the high, uneven ground that the trees populated, and into which the tracks were headed.

'Hank,' he said, 'take the ridge. If he shows, that'll maybe put him under your long gun. I'll follow the trail he's left. If we don't flush him out before sunset, we'll meet under that bluff ahead, then we'll look out for his campfire. Maybe he'll feel secure enough to make one. I'm figurin' he's under orders an' ain't cleared the country.'

Eyeing the black, craggy butte about three miles ahead, Ruger nodded and turned his horse towards the ridge. But before he left he levelled his stare on to Scallon. He said,

'Take care, y'hear?'

Scallon nodded soberly. 'You too, pardner.'

As he entered the pines, Scallon discovered they were fairly well-spaced, making riding easier than he had anticipated, but the trail was still ill-defined and complicated. It was clear the sonofabitch was continuing to be careful, even if he'd assumed there was no pursuit. Maybe, mused Scallon, their quarry had spent too many long years on owlhoot trails and just naturally laid down false sign, out of habit. But it didn't matter a damn to Scallon. He compressed his mean lips. He would keep relentlessly on. There were enough recent hoof scars to be seen on fallen, rotting timber ... twigs broken ... softer ground disturbed to make the pursuit still viable.

But the time just seemed to speed by, as if on greased wheels. Before Scallon knew it, the gloom under the trees had grown more pronounced as the last of the sun finally dropped down behind the ridge Ruger was riding.

Disappointed, Scallon paused and stared doggedly ahead, his scarred face grim. He'd been hoping to sight at least something to give fresh hope. But he'd had nary a glimpse of man, or horse. Maybe the sonofabitch had got too great a lead, maybe he and Ruger had delayed too long in Two Pines and in those rocks back there. Nevertheless, he kneed the roan on, his determination still rock solid.

A quarter of an hourlater, his frustration now rampant, he was about to turn his horse towards the butte where he'd arranged to rendezvous with Ruger, when the trees ahead began to thin out. For some reason, the discovery lifted him, sent wary anticipation tiptoeing through him. More so when the ground gradually started to shelve down to a broad, flat, grassy clearing amidst the trees.

Now, on the far side of the glade, he saw a large cabin.

Cautious excitement began to run through him at the sight of it. Was it the famed Scallon luck, come to his aid once more? No, he'd never subscribed to that fanciful idea, mostly put about by men jealous of his success. He'd always made his own luck, by suffering hardship and having a built-in cold-blooded persistence to keep on until a result was forthcoming.

He studied the cabin. Was it a line cabin of some sort, or a hideout for owlhoots? This was desolate, empty country they were in.

A tingling of anticipation began to rise in him. He held the roan in the cover of the trees and waited, his gut instincts telling him that, because of the night closing in, it would be worth biding his time.

He wasn't disappointed. Ten minutes later his hard features set as he watched three riders come in from the other side of the clearing and rein up before the cabin. He watched them dismount, listened to them boisterously joshing each other. Scallon smiled his wolf smile, which had nothing to do with humour.

It was clear the boys were in good spirits. Was the killer really so confident, that he hadn't contemplated pursuit, or thought he'd shaken it off, and was now telling his pards how he'd shot up Jenny Manners' Eatery and made Scallon bite dust?

Fading his bleak smile, Scallon stared at the trio. For sure, one of them sat a big, light bay, had a buckskin coat across the saddle, just like the gun-crazy bastard had been wearing when he had hurrahed Jenny Manners' place. Eager anticipation welled up in Scallon, sending hot needles of expectancy prickling up his backbone, causing the hair to rise on the back of his scalp.

Now he watched one of the group break off and lead the horses around the back. Behind the cabin, Scallon saw a lean-to and a stack of hay. The other two entered the cabin. Soon smoke started to rise from the stack. Scallon felt satisfaction fill him, the satisfaction he got when he knew he had run his quarry to ground, for it was clear the trio planned on staying a while. It couldn't have worked out better.

The man who had been tending to the horses now returned. He affected a swaggering gait. He opened, then slammed the cabin door loudly to behind him. More raucous noise came from inside the cabin.

Scallon narrowed his eyelids. Well, it seemed the boys were planning a high old time tonight and he'd seen enough for now. He turned the big roan and headed it towards the bluff where he'd arranged to meet Ruger.

It was near full dark by the time Ruger's low call from the rocks ahead led Scallon towards the lawman. Ruger was hunkered down eating the beef and bread Jenny Manners had pressed on them before they had left Two Pines.

Ruger's eyes narrowed as Scallon related all he knew, ending with, 'Figure I recognized his clothes and the bay.'

'Who are the others, you reckon?' Ruger asked.

In the dark, Scallon shrugged and looked bleakly across at the lawman. 'Don't know, but I reckon it's goin' to be interesting finding out.' He hunkered down. Between sips of water, he began to munch on the beef and bread he had reached out of his saddle-bag.

While he did, Ruger settled his back against a rock and rolled a quirley. 'By God, this could turn out to be quite somethin',' he said.

Scallon nodded his heartfelt agreement. 'If we can get just one of those sonsofbitches to sing....'

Ruger nodded, his round face momentarily etched by the glow of the lucifer he ignited his quirley with. He shook the match out immediately and cupped the cigarette in his horny hand to hide the glow. It was clear to Scallon the game lawman was relishing the prospect of capturing and quizzing the owlhoots down there.

And an hour later, with their horses tethered back in the trees, Scallon now crouched near the cabin. Ruger was silent and expectant beside him. They'd got close enough to hear the reedy notes of a vamped mouth-organ as it came floating away from inside the cabin and out on to the night air. Faint yellow lamplight showed through the small, bare window of the cabin. Then, abruptly, the playing stopped, somebody spoke. There followed prolonged guffaws. The playing started again and, tantalizing Scallon, there came the smell of bacon frying and the aroma of brewed coffee on the gentle breeze. Despite his having dined on cold beef, the smell was tempting.

Scallon stared through the starlight at his partner, crouched next to him. He could see the dull silver glow that was outlining the shot-gun in Ruger's ham-like right hand. He could also see the lawman's round face was shiny with sweat in the faint light.

Stirring, Scallon waved the barrel of his hand-held Colt as a signal. 'Guess it's got to be now, Hank,' he whispered. 'Take the back of the cabin. Block their getaway if they try it. I'll move in on the front.'

In acknowledgement Ruger nodded, moved off to his left.

Scallon began to move towards the cabin. Tall, lean, cat-like; his lips and throat, as usual in situations like this, were bone dry. He had a simple strategy already worked out. Go straight in, call 'hands up, or die'. After that, it would be up to the occupants to choose their destiny.

A few moments later a glance told him Ruger was now near the edge of the trees, almost parallel with the cabin. He was starting to move round the back, shot-gun held for instant action.

But the snap of a dry twig had Scallon extending his now startled stare on from Hank, and his lips drew back, almost in a frustrated snarl, when he saw what must be one of the trio walking out of the firs near Ruger, fumbling with his Levis. That sent everything haywire.

The sonofabitch immediately began yelling when he saw Ruger, 'Trouble, boys!' Then he started cursing while frantically reaching into his coat pocket. Without hand support, his Levis dropped around his ankles, exposing his filthy long johns. He looked ludicrous, but, decided Scallon, his shout wasn't.

'We're bein' raided, boys!' he was calling again. 'Rustlers!'

'Hold it,' bellowed Ruger. 'Raise your hands. I don't want to kill you.'

But the man was yanking a Colt out of his coat pocket. He raised it shakily and fired. The crashing report from it melded with the noise of Ruger's shot-gun, fired from point-blank range. The din went rampaging into the dark, silent trees.

The man gave vent to a despairing yell. His arms flared wide as he was hammered back by the savage impact of the full charge from Ruger's Parker ten-gauge. The man's own shot went clattering harmlessly through the dark branches above Ruger.

Angrily realizing it had all gone to hell, Scallon left Ruger to deal with what was left of the situation. He ran towards the cabin door. He could already hear the sound of breaking glass and anxious shouting coming from within.

By the time he burst into the stuffy cabin, he could hear hoofbeats out the back of the cabin. A swift glance around him pin-pointed the window through which the killer and his partner had made their escape.

He rushed to it and leaned out. He could faintly see the rear of two riders – one on the bay – melting into the dark trees. Ruger appeared around the corner of the cabin almost at the same time. Between them Scallon estimated they must have sent off a dozen shots.

Now Ruger, in frustration, slammed his shot-gun to the ground and glared after them. Scallon climbed out of the window by the lean-to. Then he gritted, 'Damn their hides!' To add force to Ruger's irate gesture, he threw down his own battered hat.

Ruger was still staring fiercely into the dark trees when he growled, 'Amen to that. We clean forgot about the sonofabitch guy wanting to crap.'

Having given vent to his feelings about their plan being thwarted, he picked up the shot-gun and methodically began to reload both it and his Colt. Scallon admired his professionalism and did likewise with his handgun. After that, they went to the owlhoot with his Levis around his ankles and the load of shot through his chest. The wound was an awful mess of mangled flesh and bone. It didn't need an examination to tell them he was dead.

'Know him?' Scallon asked.

Ruger nodded. 'Mel Cook. Was ridin' for the Wagon Wheel a month back. Seems he's gone to bad.' Holstering his Colt, he then said, 'What d'you think, Luke? Try an' follow them?'

Scallon scowled at the dark night. What starlight there'd been was now being covered by drifts of cloud that had started to float across the sky.

'You figure we could?' he said.

Ruger shook his head. 'Not me, for sure,' he admitted.

Scallon felt he had to be truthful, too. 'Nor me. Even I ain't *that* good.'

It was then he became reacquainted with the smell of bacon and coffee that was pervading the air. Drawn by it, Scallon walked round the cabin and stepped through the door. He could see the bacon was still sizzling in the pan on the stove and was almost on the point of burning. Its aroma was helping to kill the smell of unwashed men and clothes that clung to the place. There was also a pot of coffee on the small table alongside a pan of beans. Scallon felt both pan and pot. They were hot.

With his lop-sided grin formed, he turned to Ruger.

'You reckon we should invite ourselves to supper?'

Ruger matched his smile, seemingly

delighted to salvage at least something from the mess. 'Hell, why not? It'll sure beat the hell out of cold beef and water.'

Scallon found he couldn't agree more.

SIX

Fifteen minutes later the whinny from Scallon's roan – which he had hitched way back in the trees along with Ruger's mount while they executed the raid on the cabin – sent the manhunter rearing up from the rough table he and the lawman were sitting at. He had been wiping up the remains of the bacon fat on a tin plate he had found on the one shelf in the cabin. He had filled it with some of the beans and bacon they had found, Ruger helping himself as well. Scallon stared at the lawman, the tension lines on his face clear in the yellow lamplight.

'She's been trained,' he whispered. 'Could be trouble. Put out the light, pardner.'

Ruger, narrow-eyed, nodded, wiped bacon fat off his chin with the back of his hand before blowing down the oil-lamp funnel. It became densely dark in the small cabin.

'Out through the rear window,' hissed Scallon. 'Make for the trees. We gotta give ourselves space. In here, we're sittin' ducks.'

Ruger moved quickly in front of him, shotgun clasped in his hand. He slid silently out on to the hoof-chewed ground around the lean-to. Scallon followed him, ignoring the stabs of pain from his damaged thigh. They were sprinting for the trees when the pop of guns and the yelling of men started up behind them. Scallon immediately became aware of lead hissing viciously around him. As he ran he whistled to the roan in the trees and hoped he'd tethered her loose enough to allow her to tug free. Then, by his side, he heard Ruger gasp, falter in his stride, before he started to run again.

As they entered the trees, lead began to pepper the timber around them, rattling and humming off the boles and branches that were crowding in on them. Again Ruger started to slow up, enough to cause Scallon to put a powerful arm around him to help him on. As he did he demanded,

'You hit bad, Hank?'

'Chest.' Ruger gasped. 'Leave me. Look out for yourself.'

Scallon growled. 'To hell with that.' As he spoke he could hear more yelling behind him, then the sound of horsemen crashing into the scrub and trees.

Abruptly, Scallon stopped running. To his left, in the deep bloom, he saw a dense thicket of brush. Half-carrying Ruger, who was now grunting with pain, he forced a way into the tangle, then hit the ground, taking Ruger down with him. Breathing shallowly, he settled to wait. Ruger's breath was hissing and rattling through his clenched teeth.

It wasn't long before a horseman loomed out of the trees. They must have spread out, Scallon concluded. The rider was moving cautiously, peering into the night now silvered with starlight once more because of a gap in the clouds. He was clearly nervous and held his handgun at the ready. Automatically, Ruger and Scallon crouched lower as the rider gave the brush they were holed-up in his special scrutiny.

It was then that Scallon's big roan broke through the trees and came trotting towards their cover, stirrups flapping. Scallon tensed. Damn it, he'd trained her too good! She'd heard his 'come' whistle and she had followed her nose and done just that.

Clearly alerted by it, the rider stared around. His alarmed 'Goddamn' came to them on the still night air. He began glaring anxiously into the night, twirling his stocky piebald around to help him scan the bushes more thoroughly. He held his Colt at the ready.

'Boys,' he began bawling. 'Over here!'

Grim-faced, Scallon rose. He had to do something and damned quick. The rider was about twenty yards away. Scallon didn't hesitate. He lined up his Colt and fired.

The man yelled despairingly as Scallon's bullet knocked him out of the saddle. He hit the ground hard and lay groaning, his gun jolted out of his hand and out of reach. Now, in the distance, Scallon heard shouts getting nearer, began to hear the crash of horses pushing through the thickets towards them. Glaring into the night he said urgently, 'Hank, we gotta git out of here.'

When there was no response from the lawman, a glance down told him Ruger had passed out. He could see the dark stain of blood spreading on the starpacker's shirt. Without hesitation, he stooped and picked up the game deputy and pushed his way through the brush where they had hidden. Once out of it he whistled to the roan. She came whickering up to him.

The noises of pursuit were becoming even louder and, despite the desperate situation he was in, it puzzled Scallon. From where had the owlhoots drummed up such support so quickly? Maybe there had been a meet on, something planned … but there was no time to ponder that now. Scallon hoisted the limp form of Ruger across his horse's withers. When she smelt Ruger's blood she went white-eyed and tried to shy away. Scallon took hold of her firmly and climbed up. 'Damn you, none o' that, missy,' he hissed, and sent her into the trees. As he progressed, patiently picking his way through the tall, dark boles of firs, the sounds of the searching owlhoots gradually faded. Scallon silently thanked the sanctuary of the dark night and the crowd of trees that enveloped him.

After ten minutes of riding, Ruger moved and moaned. Scallon acknowledged Ruger's position, draped chest down over the withers as he was, must have been excruciatingly uncomfortable. It was a wonder it hadn't aroused the lawman to consciousness before now.

'Damn it, get me offen here,' Ruger gasped. 'Like fire in my chest.'

Scallon pulled the roan to a halt. He climbed down and eased Ruger off the horse, then stood holding the groggy lawman upright. He said, 'I guess, while we're about it, we'd best have a look at that wound, pardner.'

Ruger didn't complain as Scallon lowered him and propped him against a tree. Then, with careful patience, Scallon eased off the starpacker's vest and shirt. He soon established that the lead had gone clean through Ruger's body. As far as he could ascertain, with his limited knowledge of the human frame, the bullet had missed vital veins and organs, but the seeping loss of blood could be serious if it went on long enough. That much he knew.

'Gotta patch you up somehow, Hank,' he said, 'then get you to somewhere and have a real job done on you.'

'Got bandages in my saddle-bags,' gasped Ruger. 'Never ride without them.'

Scallon 'harrumphed'. It was clear Ruger hadn't fully grasped their situation yet, was maybe a little fevered. 'Just one snag to that, pardner,' he said. 'Your hoss is back yonder.'

Ruger moaned. 'Where are we?' he asked.

'Don't rightly know,' Scallon said. 'New

country to me. Readin' the stars, when I get a peek at them that is, I'd say we're headed east from the cabin. That give you any idea where we might be?'

Ruger rolled his head against the rough pine bole he was rested against and he gritted his teeth against his pain. 'From what I know, it's got to take us near to Pershay Canyon,' he gasped. 'Jenny Manners has her Circle M spread there.'

The news heartened Scallon. At least they were heading towards friends. 'That'll do, I reckon,' he said, ''til we can get to town, or get the doc out to you at the Circle M. You have a doctor in Two Pines?'

Ruger nodded. 'Doc Lancing.'

Scallon rose, went to his saddle-bags. He had two spare cotton shirts. When he reached them out, their cleanness startled him until he remembered Jenny Manners taking them from him in Two Pines. She'd said she'd have the Chinaman launder all his spare kit while he slept. Seems she had done just that. What she hadn't left in the hotel bedroom for his immediate use, she had put back in his saddle-bags.

But being a frugal man, Scallon felt the natural hurt start in him as he began to tear them up. Reminded once more of his niggardly nature he snorted his disgust. God damn it, he'd have to put his natural parsimony aside for once! Here was a true pard hurt, needful of his ministrations, and here he was railing against the necessity of ruining two shirts to do it.

Disgusted for once by his tightfistedness, he hurled his reactions to the back of his mind and soon had Ruger padded and bandaged.

Feeling good now that he had conquered his penny-pinching nature, and more at ease with himself, he stepped back and stared at his handiwork. 'Guess that should hold things for a spell,' he said.

He then eased up Ruger's head and offered him water from his canteen. The lawman drank weakly. When sated, he said, urgently, 'Leave me here, Luke. Ride on for help. Be all right 'til you get back.'

Scallon pursed his lips at that one. While he recorked the canteen and hung it on the saddlehorn he pondered on it.

Ruger's suggestion made sense of a sort, but who was to say that those sonsofbitches back there wouldn't pick up on their trail come daylight – he hadn't bothered to hide it in his hurry to get away – and find Ruger before he could get back to him? God knew what they might do to him.

'You're comin' with me, pardner,' he said. 'No arguments.' With that, he got Ruger into the saddle – sparing him pain as best he could, though Ruger didn't complain – and climbed up on to the mare's rump behind him. Supporting Ruger, he urged the big roan eastward once more.

Eventually, the trees thinned out and as dawn broke they came out on to open rangeland. From the brow of the rise where he'd paused Scallon now saw a broad canyon opening a huge gap in the broken, high country ahead. It looked a fertile place.

He could see a river coming out of it and also a yellow trail which cut a ribbon across the plain, heading south ... to Two Pines?

'Pershay Canyon,' muttered Ruger.

Looking obliquely at the lawman, sagging in the saddle in front of him, Scallon could see the starpacker's face was deathly pale. Pain etched strained lines into his usually smooth, round features.

'You figure the li'l lady'll be home?' he said.

Ruger shrugged, gasped, making it clear the move had hurt him. After moments he said, 'It'll be likely. Though she does stop over in town sometimes, she likes to be on the ranch and is in the habit of using her gig to get to town most days. She usually sets off well before dawn.'

Scallon raised brows. A remarkable lady, Jenny Manners, he thought.

He urged the roan down the long slope towards the trail. He was nearly on to it when the gig, with the handsome black in the shafts, came high-stepping out of the canyon. As soon as he was close enough he could see it was Jenny Manners sitting erect on the seat, the canopy pushed back to allow the dawn sun to shine on her and the closed duster covering her green satin dress. She was clearly at home driving the outfit. And it couldn't be missed that the latest-model Winchester was pouched in a long leather scabbard, strapped to a specially fitted bar on the rig and set at an angle so that it brought the butt near to hand, ready for instant action. When she saw him, she brought the gig to a halt and waited for him to come up.

As he drew rein beside the outfit she stared at Ruger. 'Hank?' She turned her gaze on to Scallon when she saw Ruger was only half-conscious. 'What has happened, Mr Scallon?' she demanded.

'How far is it to the ranch, ma'am?' Scallon said, ignoring her question. 'I'd like to get Hank somewhere comfortable before I go into any detail.'

A hint of colour came to Jenny Manners'

pale cheeks. She clearly viewed his brusque-
ness as a slight reprimand, but she soon
recovered when she apparently realized the
sense of it.

'Yes. Of course. Follow me.' She eased the
black around and headed back into the
canyon. Relenting a little, as they rode,
Scallon now told her what had happened
since they left her eatery yesterday. She
listened intently.

After ten minutes steady riding, Ruger
now frequently groaning his pain, Scallon
steered his roan towards the long, low,
adobe ranchhouse. As he drew close he
found it was an imposing place. It was built
on the higher ground, near the east wall of
the canyon, above the broad stream which
was lined with willows, alder and aspen. He
saw other large, neat outbuildings scattered
around it. Six-foot high pole corrals were
evident, too.

He had seen plenty of white faces amongst
the steers they'd passed, suggesting that
quality stock was bred on the Circle M.

They were scattered and grazing on the broad, green bottom of the canyon for as far as he could see.

As they got nearer he saw five hands were saddling horses, obviously making ready for the day's chores, until they saw them approach. Now they were staring curiously their way.

Drawing up in front of the stoop, Jenny Manners climbed down from the rig and called, 'Mary!' Then she turned to the inquisitive hands. 'Go about your business, boys. The story you want to hear'll be told when you get back tonight. But right now I want those steers we have held up in the North Split all branded before sundown. That doesn't give you much time.'

As she was talking a full-blood squaw came out of the ranchhouse to stand on the stoop, with hands clasped before her. Seeing her there Jenny Manners turned. Scallon met her stare. As usual, she was in calm control. 'Bring Hank into the common room, Mr Scallon,' she said, then she returned her gaze to the Indian. 'Mary, boil water and get your medicines.'

Mary Plain Blanket grunted and waddled back into the house.

Scallon eased Ruger carefully off the saddle. As he did, the lawman passed out again with a moan. Hefting him up into his arms Scallon carried him up the three steps leading to the stoop, then on into the big room beyond.

Jenny Manners, moving in front of him, said, 'Follow me.' She led him through what he judged was the common room, down a corridor, past bedrooms, and into what could only be the ranchhouse kitchen. There was a cooking range, benches, pots and pans on shelves. A long pine table stood in the centre of the room. Jenny Manners pointed to it.

'Put Hank on there, Mr Scallon,' she said. Moments later Mary Plain Blanket came in with a wooden pail of water. Expressionless, she poured the contents into a large, already half-full metal vessel on the hotplate above the wood-burning cooking range.

'I figure to ride into Two Pines, ma'am,' Scallon said as he laid Ruger on to the table. 'Call in the doc.'

Jenny Manners shook her head. 'No need for that, Mr Scallon.' She waved a hand towards the squaw. 'Mary'll beat that quack Lancing at doctoring any day of the week.'

Scallon looked doubtfully at the Indian woman – flat-faced, sullen and rotund. 'You full sure about that, ma'am?' he said.

Jenny Manners nodded. 'I am.' She turned the subject. 'Have you eaten, Mr Scallon?'

He shook his head. 'Not since last night.'

'Very well. While you attend to your horse, I'll see that something is rustled up for you.'

Scallon found himself wanting to say something, but what was there to say? Jenny Manners seemed to have things firmly in hand. He went out and unsaddled the roan, curried her, turned her into the corral and threw her hay. He'd ask about grain later. As he moved to return to the ranchhouse a rider came in from the range, passing the cowhands now moving out. Scallon stiffened. Damn it, he knew that man from way back. Drury Fuller. What was a man-killing sonofabitch the likes of him doing on Circle M land?

When he saw him, Fuller turned towards him and reined up. A seemingly warm grin spread on his smallpox-marked, sallow features. A quirley drooped from his lips. 'Howdy, Scallon,' he said, but there was no warmth in his tone, more like caution. 'Bin a long time. You got business here?'

'Could ask you the same thing,' Scallon said.

Fuller spread his arms. 'Hell, I work here.' He climbed down off his grey and hitched his gunbelt into a more comfortable position. A plain Colt was pouched in the workmanlike holster, but, Scallon knew, in Fuller's hands, it could be deadly.

'Be interesting to find out what kind of work there is for the likes of you, here on the Circle M,' said Scallon.

Fuller took the quirley stub from his

mouth and ground it into the dust. He still grinned. 'Same old Scallon. Still not an ounce of joy to be had out of you, it seems. Can't you allow a man can change?'

Scallon grunted and made off towards the ranchhouse. Inside, he was met by Jenny Manners. She directed him to a table near one of the windows in the big common room. She placed a plate of steak and eggs before him.

'Eat, Mr Scallon,' she said.

He took off his hat and placed it on the floor. 'Thank you, ma'am,' he said, then added, 'How's Hank?' He cut off a chunk of beef.

'Mary thinks he has a fifty-fifty chance. She says the way you patched him up has maybe saved his life.'

Scallon grunted, 'You trust that squaw?'

Jenny Manners stared hard at him. 'With my life.'

Scallon chewed on the steak then said, 'Fact is, I've grown to look upon Hank as a pard, ma'am. I feel I ought to go fetch out this Doc Lancing.' He was aware her green gaze was on him.

'Don't you like Indians, Mr Scallon?'

'Ain't a matter of likin',' he said. 'They just don't have the medical know-how when it comes to white man's medicine. All they practise is mumbo-jumbo.'

'On what do you base that opinion?' she demanded.

Scallon shrugged. 'Hell, word gits about. It's a known fact many In'juns are still jest one step above savages.'

'Well, I have reason to know that some white doctors are in that category, too,' retorted Jenny Manners. 'One of them, who had the gall to claim he was a surgeon no less, helped kill my father.'

Slightly shocked by the venom she put into her words, Scallon stared, a portion of steak left poised before his near lipless mouth. He could see an almost mad glaze had come to her green eyes.

'That's a powerful accusation to make, ma'am,' he said. 'You got proof?'

'Oh, yes,' she breathed. 'Want to hear it? Fifteen months ago my father took a bullet in the thigh. It needed removing. But the doctor who attended him was drunk, though he managed to hide it well. As he probed for the bullet – hardly able to see, I imagine – he cut a main artery. Within three minutes my father was dead, no matter what they did to try and save him.'

Scallon put the steak in his mouth and chewed a little before speaking. 'Well, I'm sorry to hear that, ma'am. But you can't condemn the whole medical profession because of the misconduct of one man.'

Jenny Manners stared, the mad glaze still there. 'Can't I? When the tragedy occurred I was in finishing school, back East. I returned to the ranch immediately. I had the body exhumed and I sought other medical opinion. I wanted the scoundrel struck off. But they ranked up on me, took his side. They said the position of the bullet had been such that the risk of what occurred must have been very great. They even had the audacity to say the courage the surgeon had shown in taking that risk and in trying to remove the bullet, to avoid gangrene and sure death and thus save my father's life, had been exemplary.' Her green eyes grew large and round and ever more angry. 'Exemplary! Can you believe it?'

Scallon gazed at this new Jenny Manners, at the smouldering eyes, the slightly arrogant lift of her chin.

'Well, I guess somethin' like that happenin' to kin can make a body feel bitter,' he said, but he was faintly shocked by the sudden rage that had surfaced in her, from somewhere buried deep inside of her.

She was staring at him, her green eyes now as hard as emerald.

'It's nothing to do with bitterness, Mr Scallon,' she shrilled, 'it's to do with professional incompetence and getting away with it.'

Well, that struck home with Scallon, in a roundabout way. He'd seen plenty of hard-cases get away with murder when they'd been backed up by skilful liars – some of them supposedly upright citizens, or even worse, lawyers. However, Miss Manners' fearsome prejudices aside, he'd still like to have some real medical opinion as to Ruger's chances of surviving his wound and have white treatment prescribed to achieve that end. Even so, Jenny Manners clearly wasn't a fool and, he considered, she wouldn't be easily fooled by quackery, Indian or white. So maybe the squaw did have skills. For the time being, he would have to believe that ... for Hank wanted help bad right now.

He chewed on another slice of meat. There was still another matter that was intriguing him. 'That aside, ma'am, came across Drury Fuller out yonder,' he said. 'He says he works for you.'

Jenny Manners' chin lifted again. Her stare lost its fierce glaze, but her attitude was now guarded as well as challenging. 'Have you got an objection to that?'

Scallon met her stare with equal hardness.

'Do you know he's a killer, ma'am?'

Her haughty gaze altered to one of scorn. 'These are dangerous times, Mr Scallon,' she said. 'I take whatever measures I deem necessary to ensure some sort of security. As for Fuller being tagged a killer....' her stare turned scathing as it held his own. '....I'd like to know what category you place yourself in.'

Stung, he glared, but though the raking words galled him greatly, he chose to ignore them ... for now. 'Can't the law do that?' he said. 'Give you security?'

Her lips curled, almost cynically. 'Hardly. At the moment what law we have is fighting for his life in my kitchen.'

Scallon narrowed his eyelids. He was quickly coming to the opinion that Jenny Manners was a real smart lady, formidable to anybody she decided to go up against, but there also seemed to be a certain instability as well.

He said, 'Have you been in touch with Boss Falster?'

She took off her duster and hung it on a spread of antlers. 'Yes. After three months of nagging him and that smug council they have in Rutland, Hank Ruger being placed in Two Pines was the result of that insistence.' She pushed back her long, tawny hair – running her fingers luxuriously through their auburn tresses, which gleamed with health. 'Oh, Hank's been doing an adequate job, I won't deny,' she went on, 'but he can't be everywhere at once. Now he won't be nowhere at all for quite a spell.'

Scallon sawed at the piece of steak. 'You said dangerous times for you, Miss Manners,' he probed. 'Could you enlarge on that?'

'I've already explained that briefly to you yesterday morning,' she said, impatiently. She waved a slim hand in the air. 'I've made an enemy of Stimson Randell, for one thing, and consequently most of the Cattlemen's Association. I'm a meddling woman, it seems, and Randell carries a lot of weight in the county's debating chamber. I think you've maybe already worked that out for yourself. All in all, the ranchers just don't like what I did when I settled those people on the south range.'

'So why did you?' Scallon stared at her steadily. 'You're not a fool. You must have known it wouldn't be liked.'

She sighed, appeared irritated about taking time to answer his continuous questions. She cut air with slim fingers. 'It seemed the right thing to do at the time,' she said. 'I still think it was. Men who have served their country nobly and well deserve recognition and a helping hand.'

Well, he'd never put Jenny Manners down as an idealist. She appeared too practical for that. But, then, people always had the habit of surprising him. He'd found that much out in his eventful life.

'Noble, but hardly practical, ma'am,' he said.

'Don't be so damned presumptuous,' she snapped, lifting her chin. 'It was right.' Then she sighed. 'Well, what are you going to do now, Mr Scallon?' She was clearly tired of the grilling he was subjecting her to. 'Ride on? It goes without saying, that would please me greatly.'

Once more he chose to ignore her barbs. He said, 'Fact is, far as I know, I'm still a deputized lawman, Miss Manners. And complicating things for me – as far as leavin' is concerned – a member of the county force and a friend to boot, has been brutally shot down and is near to death in your kitchen. I shall report that fact to Boss Falster. It'll be then up to him to say whether or not he wants me to continue to work as a deputy around here while Hank recuperates. It won't suit my nature – I like to keep moving – but I've sure got a burning ambition to help bring those responsible for Hank's hurts and Jimmy Blue's death to justice.'

Her stare was scornful as it held his. 'No fat rewards to lure you away to some other place?' she said. 'Makes me wonder what

Stimson Randell has in mind for you when he gets you to the Wagon Wheel to pay you. More dollars for more blood?'

That did it. Scallon tightened his grip on the knife and fork he was holding. His knuckles showed white before he slowly laid the cutlery down into the bloody gravy the half-eaten steak and broken egg yolks were swimming in. Then he turned his bleak gaze fully on to her as he rose from the table.

He couldn't help but growl, 'For that, ma'am, if you weren't a growed woman with a heap of responsibility on your shoulders and a heap of face to uphold around here, I'd spank you so hard you'd scream for mercy.' He stooped and picked up his hat and walked past her into the kitchen.

He found Hank Ruger was still on the table. He appeared to be unconscious. The squaw had obviously cleaned up and doctored the wound. It was now expertly bandaged up. The Indian was tidying up the salves and potions she had used to do the job. Now she picked up the bucket of warm, bloody water by the side of the table and stepped out the back to empty it.

When she came back she said, 'Lawman sleep.' As she spoke her dark, fathomless eyes gazed into his own. 'Give him medicine for that. Long time before him better. But, if strong man like I think, he make it, maybe.' Now she pointed. 'Ask lady boss where to put him. But tell her him must not travel far for long time.' She bustled out of the room, carrying her medicaments.

Scallon turned. Jenny Manners was standing in the doorway. 'You heard her?' he said.

'Yes.' She stepped into the room. For once, she looked pale and uncertain. 'I'm sorry. What I said back there was wrong and unnecessary.'

He glared at her. He was in no mood for apologies. 'It was said. Now, what about Hank? He can't travel yet.'

She soon recovered her self-assured demeanour after lowering it a moment to apologize. She tilted her chin. 'I'll put him in Father's room. Mary can prepare it.' As if to explain she added, with a slight catch in her voice, 'It has been closed up since he died.'

The mention of her father again aroused Scallon's curiosity. He felt compelled to ask, 'How long did you say your father's been dead? You run this place on your own?'

She stared at him. 'You have a million questions, don't you, Mr Scallon?'

'Part of my trade,' he grunted.

She moved to the big cupboard close by and ran her hand along the plain wood. 'As I said, he has been dead fifteen months,' she said. 'The reason why he is dead, I have explained.' She paused, tightened her lips and clasped her hands in her lap. Then she raised her brows. Her hesitancy indicated to Scallon she was clearly debating whether to carry on. Finally she said, 'Mother died seven years ago. My brother, Sean, was killed at Antietam. My older sister, Sarah, is married, has three children and lives in St Louis. My other brother died of pneumonia when he was eight, right here on this ranch.' Her green stare now fastened on to him defiantly. 'There, you have my family history in a nutshell, Mr Scallon, and why I have to run the place on my own.'

'I didn't ask for such intimate detail.'

She laughed, throatily. 'No, you didn't. But you are not sorry I gave it to you.'

Choosing to ignore the suggestion that he was constantly prying he said, 'Why don't you get in a manager? It'll leave you free to run your hotel and eatery.'

'At the moment, I prefer to run things myself.'

'How did your father come to get shot?'

'He was chasing rustlers.'

'The problems on this range ain't new, then,' Scallon said.

'No.'

Scallon nodded, stared at the pretty Circle M owner. Though she still looked composed, he sensed an anxious tightness about Miss Jenny Manners. In fact, he had done so since he'd first come in contact with her, though she hid it well. Was she finding the going was beginning to get too tough for her, hence Drury Fuller?

He pursed his lips. 'Well, thank you for your candour, ma'am. I guess I'll get back to town when I've seen Hank put to bed.'

Judging by the way her green stare hardened, she seemed to take exception to that. 'We have hands quite capable of lifting the deputy, Mr Scallon.'

'I'm sure,' he admitted. 'But, if you don't mind, I want to see a job through. Now, I'd like to grain my horse. Have I your permiss...?'

'Company.' Intruding, the brisk, shouted call came from outside. Scallon recognized Drury Fuller's gruff tones.

Jenny Manners' green gaze turned to him. It was puzzled, as well as worried. With her he made his way to the front of the ranchhouse.

SEVEN

Outside, Scallon found Drury Fuller was lounging on the long tie rail fronting the stoop. He was watching five riders splashing across the broad, deep stream that drifted past the ranch about a quarter of a mile away. They now began to move up the gentle slope to the house.

To Scallon, even at this distance, they looked hardcases to a man. And as they drew closer Scallon immediately recognized the light bay and the clothes on the man riding it. The same man who had been at the cabin last night and yesterday had shot up Jenny's Eatery and killed Jimmy Blue, or he'd eat his hat.

His strong jaw set and his mean stare hardened. He loosened his Colt. A glance to his side told him Jenny Manners had a

Winchester in her hand, probably the one he had seen placed strategically on a gun rack, near the ranchhouse door. She held it with assurance. Well, he already knew she was not afraid to use it. But it was her sharp intake of breath that really made him stare at her.

'Know them?' he asked.

'The one on the bay is Stimson Randell's son, Carder Randell, the tall lean one next to him is the Wagon Wheel straw boss, Charlie Gratton.' Then she shook her head. 'The other three … no, but I know the type. Hired more for their ability with guns than their skill in handling livestock.'

Scallon narrowed his gaze and stared at the incoming group. 'You say that's Stimson Randell's son on the bay?'

'The same,' said Jenny Manners. 'I half-guessed it was him yesterday, despite the bandanna he was wearing, but couldn't bring myself to believe it.'

Scallon set his chin. That news opened a whole new can of worms.

Drury Fuller, quirley drooping from his mouth, began to move to the very end of the tie rail. As he did so he said, 'I'll take flank, Scallon.'

Though it galled him to agree, Scallon nodded. 'Be useful.' Then he said to Jenny Manners, 'What do you know of Carder Randell?'

Jenny's emerald stare was hard. 'Browbeaten, but, in contradiction, also spoilt to death by his father, after his mother died ten years ago. Now grown, Carder's got to believe he can ride roughshod over anybody he chooses to, his father being the power he is around here. Got so bad lately, Stimson's now grudgingly recognized his earlier mistakes and has made Charlie Gratton responsible for Carder, to try and keep him in line. Make him grow up.'

'And Gratton undertook to do that?' asked Scallon, slightly surprised.

'Gratton has a wife and family to provide for. He'd sooner do that, I guess, than risk losing his job. Though, I reckon, there's a limit to his patience.'

When the riders drew up they spread out into a line. The tall, aquiline-featured rider at its centre leaned forward, rested his hands on the saddle horn. Grey salted what dark hair Scallon could see poking out from under his hat. The man touched the brim of his black Stetson.

'Miss Manners.'

Jenny Manners turned. 'Mr Scallon,' she said, 'meet Charlie Gratton, Stimson Randell's straw boss.' She returned her stare to the rider. 'Well, what's on your mind, Charlie? You're way off your home range here.'

But Carder Randell leaned forward – big, aggressive and handsome with his long blond hair and blue eyes. He waved a hand. He yelled, 'Go on, tell her, Charlie.' Then he grinned, denying what Scallon thought was anger in him. 'We got you good now, Jenny "high an' mighty" Manners,' he crowed. 'You've rode heavy over me an' Pa once too often.'

As if tiredly, Charlie Gratton drifted a warning gaze on to the young Randell. 'Shut it, will you, boy?'

Carder Randell glared. 'Who the hell are you callin' boy? An' who the hell are you to tell me to shut it?' he growled viciously. He pointed a long finger at the straw boss. 'Gratton, I'm gittin' sick an' tired of you pushin' me around – of havin' to take your orders.' He swung his point on to Jenny. 'An' I'm gettin' tired of that bitch lookin' at me as though I'm some kind of dirt every time she sees me.'

'You ask for it,' Gratton growled. 'An' you'll take orders from me until your pa says otherwise. An' that can't come too damned quick fer me.'

With that, Gratton turned. His taciturn face revealed nothing as he glanced warily at Drury Fuller, who was smiling at him from his position at the end of the rail.

'Followed tracks out of the badlands, Miss Manners,' Gratton said. 'They ended up here.' The Wagon Wheel straw boss narrowed his eyelids. 'Fact is, one of our hands has been killed back there, ma'am, another injured bad. We have reason to believe the killers came this way.'

'That's a coincidence,' said Jenny Manners sweetly. 'Mr Scallon here has just recently brought in Deputy Sheriff Hank Ruger, badly shot up, also from "back there" as you put it. They had been on the trail of a man wanted for murder in Two Pines. Mr Scallon here says when they ran him to ground they discovered he was in the company of other men. In the prosecution of their duty, shots were exchanged. During the encounter, one of them was killed. The other, with the killer, escaped. Later, they were set upon by other riders and had to return fire. Mr Scallon and the deputy were lucky to escape with their lives. In fact Deputy Ruger's life still hangs in the balance, shot through as he is.'

As Jenny spoke Scallon caught the straw boss's steely glance as it turned on to him. 'Scallon, huh?' Gratton said, ignoring Jenny

Manners for the moment. 'The boss's been expecting you.'

Carder Randell mumbled, his blue stare icy, 'Yeah. Where the hell you been, Scallon?'

Ignoring Randell, Scallon turned to the straw boss. 'As you just heard, got delayed, Gratton. Fact of the matter is' – he pointed – 'that sonofabitch on the bay ... he just happens to be the bastard we're after.'

With blurring movement he drew his Colt and lined it up, cocking the hammer as he did. He'd long since established that attack was the best form of defence. The trick was to maintain it.

The speed of the draw brought a rumble of surprised alarm from the gathered riders. Hands swooped for gunmetal, then froze as more ominous clicks came from another trigger hammer being thumbed full back. Though he didn't look, Scallon knew it was Drury Fuller.

'That's as far as your play goes, boys,' Fuller drawled, from his position at the end of the tie rail. 'Just keep your guns where they are.'

Jenny Manners raised her Winchester and sighted it up. 'Good advice,' she said, 'and to confirm what you say about the bay, Mr Scallon, I'd know it anywhere, and the clothes the man is wearing.'

Scallon grinned. 'Well, I guess a woman would notice those things.'

Charlie Gratton's gaze turned to slits of steel. 'By God, ma'am, what the hell you think you're sayin'? We've just buried a Wagon Wheel hand back there – blown apart by a ten-gauge – packed another man back to the ranch badly wounded. Now you come accusin' Carder of a killin'. You gone out of your mind? This range is dangerous enough, without addin' to it.'

Jenny Manners said, 'My mind is sound, Charlie. The fact is Carder shot up the front of my café yesterday. In the course of the attack, Jimmy Blue was killed. Maybe not intentionally, but he was.' She turned her stare on to the young Randell. 'It's not me

134

that's going out of my mind, Charlie, it's him.'

Also wanting to state his piece, Scallon drew himself up to his full six-feet three inches. 'Not only that, he shot a sworn-in lawman in the leg. Me.' He held his cold gaze on the straw boss. 'Gratton, here's how it went. After the shootin' up of Jenny's café, me an' Deputy Ruger trailed the killer of Jimmy Blue. His tracks led us to the cabin back there. There it was discovered the sonofabitch also had two other men with him. When I recognized the bay he was riding and the clothes he was wearin', I reckoned I'd seen enough.'

Though clearly uncomfortable with the news, Gratton glared and roared, 'Carder was on Wagon Wheel range all yesterday. Nowhere near Two Pines.'

Scallon ignored his protest and continued, 'In the attempt to arrest the killer, Deputy Ruger was forced to shoot your man, in defence of his own person. Later, while investigatin' the cabin, we were set upon by riders comin' out of the night. Deputy Sheriff Hank Ruger was badly wounded in the attack. Are you the people who attacked us?'

Gratton made a scoffing noise and rocked in the saddle. 'Attacked you?' he growled, his gaze slits of steel. 'Well, see how this fits an' how it was. I sent Carder on with two hands to that cabin to prepare supper' – he turned to Jenny – 'you know the one I mean. The one the Wagon Wheel uses when brandin' in Coon Valley. Next I know Carder an' the other hand left alive come ridin' in hell-for-leather. Straight off they went on about the shootin' at the cabin. So, sure, we rode in. Sure, we shot up the place. We figured whoever it was had to be rustlers. Now, damn it, I have a man dead back there, another injured. What have you got to say to that?'

Scallon stared at the straw boss. Either the man was a rank liar, or … could it be he was telling the truth? But, damn it, it didn't fit.

'Well, I ain't in the habit of callin' a man a

liar, Gratton, until I know for sure he is, so I won't. But this is how it happened for me an' Hank Ruger. We'd come upon the man we had been trailin'. His horse and his dress gave him away. Somehow, he'd got reinforcements and when, as officers of the law, we moved to apprehend the suspect things ran right out of hand.'

Now Scallon turned his gaze on to the arrogant-looking younger Randell sitting on the bay and glaring at him. He added, formally, 'And until that can be proven otherwise…. Carder Randell, you're comin' into Two Pines with me. The charge is unlawful use of guns on the streets and murder.'

Carder Randell's face widened with utter surprise for a moment before he let out a scoffing guffaw. When it subsided he said, 'You gone plumb crazy, or somethin'?'

Charlie Gratton waved a gloved hand to silence Carder. His lean, hawk face went red and mean, his stare changed to resemble two pebbles of the hardest granite. He moved his hand towards his Colt. 'Lissen good, Scallon, you ain't takin' that man nowhere, y'hear? You realize this is the Wagon Wheel you're buckin'?'

Scallon returned the straw boss's stony glare. 'Gratton, you'd be advised not to obstruct an officer of the law and to ride out. Randell will have his day in court. No doubt his father will lay on smart lawyers. As regards your own version of what happened out there in the hills ... you can do your testifyin' on the day the court convenes. Me an' Hank'll be ready.'

Gratton glowered from under dark, bushy brows. 'Let Carder go with *you?*' he said as if disbelieving Scallon. 'Have him backshot on the way in?' The straw boss reared tall in the saddle. 'Well, to hell with that. What I heard, you got a reputation, mister. An', hell, for sure, you ain't no lawman.'

Scallon remained cool. He'd learnt long ago to do that. 'You've been listenin' to far too many barroom tales, Gratton. If you take the trouble to study my real record, you'll find I've never backshot a man in my life. Whoever I have shot, he was always facin' front an' shootin' back. Now, go back an' tell Stimson Randell his boy will stand trial in Two Pines just as soon as we can get a judge an' jury to deal with it.'

Gratton swung his steely stare off Scallon and on to Jenny Manners. 'You goin' to stay a party to this?'

Jenny Manners lifted her round chin. She leaned forward, her small, oval face intent. 'What's the matter, Charlie?' she said. 'You telling me the Wagon Wheel's afraid of a little real law when it meets up with it?'

Gratton's brows shot up. 'Real law?' scoffed the straw boss. 'From that damned bounty hunter?'

Still sighting down the rifle Jenny Manners countered firmly, 'Sworn in by Boss Falster, on Stimson Randell's say-so.'

Gratton reared up in the saddle and glared. Anger darkened his aquiline features. 'Way I heard it, on'y while he rounded up Ben Hagler, damn it.'

'Nevertheless, the fact is, Stimson still seems keen to use his talents for something,' went on Jenny coolly. 'He's proved that by sending for him. But for what? Ben Hagler's dead.'

Gratton scowled darkly and moved uncomfortably in the saddle. After moments he growled, 'You figure you're real smart don't you, missy? Well, if you want an answer to that one you'd better ride over and ask Randell yourself.'

Jenny Manners smiled. 'Don't think that would be wise right now, Charlie.' Then her grin faded. She waved the rifle. 'Now, get off my land.'

Gratton stayed put, his grey stare hard. 'I'll say it agin, ma'am. If you take sides on this, you'll be makin' the biggest mistake of your life.'

'*Me* making a mistake, Charlie,' countered Jenny, 'siding with the law as it stands? You trying to say I'm doing wrong in that?'

Gratton narrowed his eyelids. He moved angrily in the saddle while an ice-cold aura of menace seemed to grow in him. He rasped, 'You're damned smart, Miss Manners, no denyin' that. But maybe you're gettin' too smart. Come on, boys ... Carder.'

Gratton tugged around the big grey he was riding. The Wagon Wheel riders did likewise, but the crack of Scallon's Colt stopped every man in his tracks.

He said evenly, 'Hold it, boys ... Randell, you're goin' nowhere. Climb down, you're under arrest.'

Disbelief now shadowed Carder Randell's handsome features. He stared anxiously at the Wagon Wheel straw boss. His face was red with anger and for the first time, Scallon could see that the bluff arrogance that had been on it had been wiped off. 'Charlie,' Randell hissed, 'fer God's sake, you gotta do somethin'. Pa pays you fer that.'

Gratton eased his grey to a stop and turned it round again. His lean face was tired and hollow as he stared at the young Randell. Then he eyed the three guns lined up on him.

Scallon decided to prod him. 'So it's make your mind up time, Charlie. But just remember, if you do start some play, you'll be first. I guarantee it.'

Gratton's bleak stare was pure steel this time. He leaned forward. 'You figure you're a real hero, huh, bounty hunter?'

Scallon shrugged, smiled lazily. 'Jus' doin' my job.'

Gratton swung his gaze on to the young Randell. 'Don't worry, boy, your pa will get you out. Rest easy in that cell they put you in. You won't be there long.'

'Hell, can't we do something now?' Carder Randell's demand was harsh. 'Damn it, we're five to three here.'

Gratton glowered, stared across the line of menacing guns pointed at him, before switching his gaze to Randell once more. 'You figure to open the play, Carder?' he demanded. His voice was heavy with sarcasm.

Randell pulled a face, flushed. 'Hell,' he blustered, 'shows where you're goin' to come from in a real fight. It's down to me, huh? Well, I ain't afraid to pull.' He glared at the other three hardcases. 'You with me, boys?'

Alarm flared through Scallon. He tensed as did Fuller and Jenny, still beside him. But Gratton raised his hand and called,

'Hold it, men!' The straw boss's urgent command was harsh. Then a tired, bleak smile touched his lips before he said, contemptuously, 'You're all mouth an' no brain, Carder.' Then his features hardened once more. 'I've told you, we'll git you out. So cool it. Rest easy.'

With that he swung his grey, quirted it, and headed up the canyon. Raising their dust, the Wagon Wheel riders closed in behind him.

Cursing, Carder Randell glared after them before dismounting slowly and staring at the guns trained on him. Then he gazed at Jenny. 'You figure you're goin' to get away with this, you crazy bitch?' he growled. 'An', by God, to think Pa thought at one time we might hitch up together – unite the Wagon Wheel with the Circle M. Well, you were allus too high-nosed fer me, an' I told him. An' since you come back from that fancy school, Pa says you've got to be nothin' but a pain in the ass.'

Nothing on Jenny Manners' face gave the impression that she was mad or amused. She merely said, 'Well, your pa allus did have a way with words.'

When Randell was afoot, Fuller moved quickly to him. He removed the young rancher's Colt, then frisked him. A thin smile spread across Fuller's lips as he discovered what the search revealed. He removed a Colt Sheriff from Carder's shoulder holster, a Green River knife from the sheath across his back, under his coat. Then Fuller withdrew the Winchester, pouched in Randell's saddle scabbard. He dumped the lot on the stoop. They clattered with loud noise on to the boards.

'Quite a little armoury, Randell,' Scallon said.

Carder scowled. 'Your damned hide won't be worth a plugged nickel when Pa gets to hear 'bout this, you know that?'

Scallon smiled, but said nothing.

Meantime, Jenny Manners had lowered her Winchester. She said to Fuller, 'Well, tie him up, Drury, ready for taking into Two Pines.'

'Will do, ma'am.' Scallon met Fuller's gaze as it turned to him. 'Just keep your gun on him while I stir up some rope.'

It was a reasonable request and Scallon accepted it as such.

EIGHT

As he rode along, Scallon scowled sourly up at the brassy sky, then wiped sweat, made muddy by the rising dust, off his brow with a big hand. The rays of the near noon-high sun were so frying hot now they were burning through his vest and shirt like a branding iron.

He stared ahead to Jenny Manners, shaded by the pulled up canopy on the gig, which she handled with such ease. She'd elected to ride into Two Pines with him, as he escorted Randell to the jail there. She was moving it briskly along in front of them, using occasional sharp snaps of the whip that ended near the high-stepping, handsome black's ears. Scallon rode his now grain-fed roan – courtesy of the Circle M – keeping it behind Carder Randell's bay. The

146

rancher's son had his arms bound to his sides. He rode stiffly and silently on the bay, as if unaware of the hot sun, his wide-brimmed hat affording him some shade.

Before they had left the ranch, Jenny had instructed Drury Fuller to keep an eye open around the place. She'd said that Hank Ruger, like herself and Scallon, were key witnesses. There'd be no telling what lengths the Wagon Wheel boss would go to to get Carder free and exact revenge, she'd added.

Riding along, Scallon felt he could easily endorse that opinion, having had experience of Stimson Randell's ruthless side. And there was the possibility the elder Randell would be fretting about what Carder might let out during his incarceration if pushed – that is if he knew anything at all. But Scallon had got the distinct impression, from recent information, that Carder was proving to be a disappointment to Stimson Randell. Maybe he hadn't yet let his son in on his shadier deals, if there were any, of course.

But there was another puzzling thing

about the events just gone: had the order to shoot up Jenny's place actually come from the elder Randell? If so, why had he given the job to his apparently weak son, of all people? Mystified, Scallon shook his head. And why attempt to shoot him, Luke Scallon, when Stimson Randell had appeared so keen to employ him once more? Or was it just a coincidence he'd happened to be in the café and had got in the way? Jenny Manners had already suggested that the shooting could well have been nothing to do with him and everything to do with her. Yes, thought Scallon. Maybe Randell had wanted to put the frighteners on Jenny Manners. She had certainly crossed him by helping those people to settle on the south range. But to send his son to do the job ... that took some believing, unless he was testing him. And that didn't seem likely, either. He kneed the roan alongside Jenny's gig.

'What's it between you an' Stimson Randell?'

She gave him a long, cold look, then said, 'More questions, Mr Scallon?' Then she shrugged. 'Well, it goes back some way. Our ranges adjoin, you see. Together they'd make the largest and best ranch holding on the range, if not the Territory. Stimson would like to buy me out, seeing as marriage was never even a starter between Carder and me. But there's one thing he fails to appreciate: I have plans of my own.'

Scallon said, 'Like helping settlers take over his south range?'

Her stare was sharp and fierce. 'He has no claim to that land.'

'But you knew it would needle him.'

She didn't reply, just kept in the shade of the gig's canopy.

'What about the rustlin' that's goin' on?' Scallon said. 'Some say Stimson Randell's been hit harder than most.'

Her gaze, when it turned to him, was neutral. She shrugged her slim shoulders. 'We've all taken losses. He's not on his own there. Maybe he's more vulnerable, where he is. A lot of his range borders the badlands. Coon Valley, for instance. Maybe that's the reason.'

Scallon muttered, 'Maybe.' He dropped back again. Seemed he'd landed in the middle of a power struggle of sorts, but he didn't dwell on it.

Half an hour later, the trio's mid-afternoon progress down Two Pines main street caused a fantastic amount of interest. And as Scallon turned for the law office, Jenny urged the black towards the livery stables.

Scallon dismounted at the law office tie rail, poked Randell through the crowd with his Colt and guided him up on to the boardwalk. With the keys Hank had handed over to him he soon had the office door open. Before giving him the keys, the plucky deputy had attempted to rise from his sickbed and come into town with him, but the weakness in him, brought on by the considerable amount of blood he'd lost, proved too much. With a gasp of defeat he'd sunk back on to the pillows.

Inside the hoosegow, Scallon shut out the crowd, telling them to go home, then undid the rope around Randell's chest. Without ceremony he shoved him into one of the two cells at the back of the brick building and locked the door. Randell had taken the rough handling stoically, a mirthless smile on his lips. But now, in the cell, he turned and stared at Scallon with blazing blue eyes. His lip-curled sneer revealed even teeth.

'You ain't got a prayer,' he breathed. 'You know that?'

Scallon smiled. 'Your pa put you up to that shootin' yesterday?'

Randell continued to gaze, the sneer still on his face. 'I surely don't know what you're talking about, mister,' he purred. 'I was on Wagon Wheel range all yesterday, like Charlie Gratton said. Ask any of the boys.'

Scallon grinned. 'May just do that. They can't all be liars.'

'They've no need to be,' said Randell.

Scallon refrained from answering the

151

cocky rancher's son. He locked the cell and left Randell lying on the wooden bench that also served as a bed. He was grinning contemptuously at Scallon.

Back in the small office Scallon found a star and hooked it on. He should at least look the part, he decided. Then he went outside and led his own roan and Randell's bay down to the livery stable. He left them with the friendly hostler. While in the livery he saw that Jenny Manners' gig was parked on the back lot. The hostler was grooming the black. Its coat was already shining with health.

He was walking up the boardwalk past Randell's Hotel, the sign bearing the slogan *first class service always*, when three men rose from the seats outside and barred his way. They were clearly rangemen.

He came to a stop and eyed them coldly. 'Gents? Something on your minds?'

The burly one with the bow legs and sad moustache stared at him with mournful eyes. 'You jus' brought in Carder Randell.

Mebbe that not good t'ing.'

Scallon narrowed his eyelids. 'What's it to you?'

The solid-looking man with the flat Caucasian features shrugged. 'Mebbe plenty.'

Scallon stared at him. 'You care to elaborate?'

The spokesman stared with his big, brown, solemn eyes. 'Stimson Randell – he go crazy vhen he find out, you bet. Damn, mister, you brought enough trouble to Two Pines already. Now you vant to bring more?'

'Carder Randell has broken the law,' Scallon said coolly. 'He'll have to stand trial for that. Now, move aside, gents.'

'Vhat he done that so bad?' demanded the spokesman.

'If you want to know that, be at the trial.' Scallon made ready to move past them.

The three men still stood their ground. The burly spokesman said, 'You know who I am, mister?'

Scallon shook his head. A warmth of anger was beginning to stir in him, due to their persistent obstruction. 'No,' he said. 'And it wouldn't make a damned bit of difference if I did. You got that?'

'Vell, mister, I'm Carl Jensen. I own the Crossed Keys, south-west of here. These are two of my boys, Richard and Johann.'

Scallon nodded, eyed the two flanking their father. 'Gents.'

The Crossed Keys owner went on, 'The Cattlemen's Association vill take a dim view of this, mister, I tell you now.'

'They the law hereabouts?'

Jensen scowled. 'You know vhat I mean.'

Scallon frowned, as if he was confused. 'They got strings they can pull, or somethin'?'

Jensen sighed. 'You not bein' helpful, mister. Me and my boys – ve're tryin' to help you. Stimson Randell, he can be a mean man.'

Scallon raised dark brows. 'That so? Well, I ain't here to be helpful, or to be helped. Just here to uphold the law.'

Richard Jensen, unlike his father, was tall

and rangy. He mumbled in good American, 'You ain't no damned lawman.'

'I am 'til I'm told otherwise,' said Scallon.

'Rumour has it you brought in Carder fer that shootin' at Jenny's yesterday.'

'Rumour has it right.'

'You must be out of your mind,' Richard Jensen growled. 'Ain' no sense to it. Why in the hell would Carder go an' do a thing like that?'

'That's puzzlin' me a little,' admitted Scallon.

Carl Jensen's dark, bushy brows shot up triumphantly. 'You see. Even you. You not sure.'

Scallon allowed himself one of his grimacing, lopsided smiles. 'Oh, I'm sure he did it. Just ain't sure *why* he did it. Day gents.'

Old man Jensen said, 'You silly man, Mr Scallon. You know that? Stimson Randell ... he get you if you don't let his boy go.'

Scallon walked past them, up the boardwalk.

At the telegraph office, he wired Sheriff Boss Falster, then asked how long the reply would take.

'Depends on how fast the operator can move, and the recipient takes to reply,' came the caustic return from the thin, consumptive-looking operator.

Scallon glared for a moment. 'You figure? Well, let's see how fast you can move when you bring the response, mister. I'll be in the law office.'

The answer took three hours to come through. Scallon read it, his face grim. It was terse and to the point. RANDELL'S PUT UP BAIL STOP LET CARDER OUT STOP HE'LL STAND TRIAL HERE STOP LIKE YOU TO CONTINUE TO COVER FOR RUGER STOP FALSTER.

Scallon scowled and crumpled the wire up in his big hand. Frustration churned through him. Let Carder Randell go? God damn! But at least Falster must have stood his ground with regard to keeping him,

Scallon, on to cover the law here at Two Pines. Must have been quite a feat to get Stimson Randell and the council to agree to that after he'd put their boy in jail.

He picked up the ring of keys lying on the desk. He stared at them for a moment with hard eyes. But it had to be done.

Scallon watched Carder Randell's grin widen slowly as he undid the cell door and swung it open.

'You're free to go, Randell,' he said. 'Your father's put up bail. Git back to the Wagon Wheel an' stay there. You're to stand trial in Rutland.'

Delight spread across Randell's handsome face. 'So soon?' he crowed. 'Well, Pa never was one to hang around.'

He sauntered out. Arrogant contempt showed on every line of his face. As he was about to go past Scallon grabbed him by the shirt collar, right at the neck, and drew him close. 'Listen good, you bastard,' he hissed in his ear. 'Git the hell out of this town pronto. Just try one damned thing an' I'll beat the shit right out of you.'

Carder's blue eyes hardened to steel, for the first time. He growled, 'Mister, you've got this whole thing wrong. It was like Charlie Gratton said. I know nothin' about shootin' up Jenny Manners' place.'

Scallon let him loose. Randell grinned, while rubbing his neck. 'Now, jest give me my guns an' my hoss, bounty hunter, an' I'll be on my way.'

'Into the office.' Scallon shoved him forward.

Still grinning, Randell soon had his gun rig snugly buckled around his hips. He adjusted it to suit, then he strapped on the shoulder holster and slipped in the Colt Sheriff. Then he slid his big knife into the sheath still set across his back. After that he drew on his fancy buckskin coat. Finally, he picked up the Winchester. He hefted it.

'That jest leaves the horse, bounty hunter,' he said.

Scallon glared. 'Down at the livery.'

Still smiling, Randell strolled out on to the

boardwalk. There he stopped. 'How about just one leetle drink before I go ... at Pa's place?'

'Git, God damn you,' snarled Scallon, 'an' don't stop until you reach the Wagon Wheel.'

Still grinning, Randell went down the boardwalk.

Before he went after him, Scallon stared at the shattered front of Jenny's Eatery across the street. Two men had just about finished repairing it. He wasn't surprised to see Jenny Manners come bolting out of the door and make towards him while staring at Randell's back as he strolled down the street.

'Have you gone crazy?' she demanded when she reached his side.

Scallon scowled and shoved the wire into her hand. 'I take it you can read.'

As she scanned the sheet what anger there was in her melted down to disbelief. Her green gaze was round when it once more tangled with his own bleak look.

'What a mockery that trial will be,' she said.

'You reckon that too, huh?'

'Can't you do something?' she demanded.

'Wave a wand, mebbe?' he snapped caustically.

He started to walk down the street. Passing Randell's Hotel he saw the Jensens were still seated out front, drinking beer. They grinned as he went past. Johann raised his glass.

'You see how it vorks on this range, mister?' old man Jensen jeered.

'An' you're happy with that?' snarled Scallon. He felt he had to lash out at somebody. 'You happy that Jimmy Blue is dead because of that sonofabitch – that Jenny Manners' café front has been blown apart?'

'We know vitch side our bread is buttered, mister,' nodded Jensen. 'You bet.'

But Johann moved uneasily in his seat. 'Carder's no good, Pa. You know it. It's time he was taken down a peg.'

Old man Jensen glared. 'You vatch your mouth, Johann.' He tapped his barrel chest with a thick finger before he waggled it. 'Your poppa knows vhat is good for us. You see.'

Scallon left them arguing. At least it seemed there was some dissent concerning the Randells.

At the livery he found Randell was saddling up. 'Don't I git to get some vittles?' he griped as soon as Scallon came through the door. 'It's a four hour ride to the Wagon Wheel. Ain't eaten since last night. An' I gotta say it – despite her bein' a bitch – Jenny still fixes the best steak in town.'

Scallon stared bleakly. Was there no end to his conceit? 'Mister, you're thinnin' my patience to nil. You got just two minutes.'

Carder grinned. 'Well, Pa said you were mean ... just what he wanted.' With that he secured the cinch and climbed up. He even tipped his hat. '*Adios*, Scallon. Can't say it's been a pleasure.'

Scallon moved out with the young

Randell, out on to the dusty street. Though it was late afternoon, Scallon found the heat of the sun still strong enough to scorch his shoulders, but he hardly noticed. He watched Randell heel the bay and send it cantering up the street towards the hills. Carder Randell wasn't much more than a dot on the horizon when Scallon turned and headed for the office once more.

But as he turned to walk back up the street, he thought it was more than a coincidence when a rider spurred out of one of the side streets ahead and pounded down the trail that led to Jenny Manners' Circle M spread. Was Jenny Manners sending a man out to warn Drury Fuller to bring in the hands and expect trouble?

Scallon's face grew long and thoughtful as he stared after the rider's dust.

NINE

Scallon twirled the pen in his hand before setting it down on the scarred desk. He'd been writing up the day's log in Ruger's neat record book. Now he stared out of the law office window at the dark street. Being near to midnight, the day's heat was long dead. A cool breeze was coming in from the hills beyond the town. It moaned through the gaps in the wooden awning over the boardwalk outside. The only other sound was the out-of-tune piano still jangling at John's Place.

Hunger pangs were biting at his flat stomach. He raised thin brows. He should have eaten at Jenny Manners' earlier, but hadn't. Now it was far too late. The lights in the café had been extinguished long ago. But the Circle M owner must still be in town, he decided. He hadn't seen the gig go past and he'd been looking.

He rose and reached for his hat hanging on the peg behind the swivel chair. He tugged it on and bent to blow out the lamp. He'd make a tour of the town before he used one of the benches in the two cells for sleep.

But the shattering of glass, the slapping of lead into the far wall and the accompanying boom of a rifle sent him to the floor and crawling for the door. Reaching it, he opened it slightly. Again the rifle boomed. He saw the gun-flash in the mouth of the alley across the street. Lead thumped into the jamb above his head.

Cursing, he slammed the door to. He crawled to the desk, reached up for the lamp, pulled it down and blew it out. More lead savaged the office.

He drew his Colt and lined up on the alley. He whacked off two shots. The reply came instantly: three more angry shots, but badly aimed. Well, decided Scallon, grim thankfulness flooding through him, whoever it was over there wouldn't win any prizes for marksmanship. If the man had had any ability at all Scallon knew he should have been dead immediately after that first shot came through the window, silhouetted as he had been by the lamplight.

And, with indecent speed, one name did spring to mind. Carder Randell. No, couldn't be. Randell had to be a better shot than that. Stimson Randell would have seen to that. But it still remained a possibility. Young Randell had the arrogance. Scallon glowered bleakly at the dark mouth of the alley. Resolve began to fill him. One thing he had to do, he had to capture the rifleman, start getting some answers.

He racked his brains. Then he remembered. There was a door that led out to the alley at the back. He reached up for the ring of keys on the desk. He was now itching to know who the bushwhacker was, itching to know who'd sent him, too.

To keep the bushwhacker interested, he sent off two more shots towards the alley, then swiftly reloaded as more lead answered him. He fired again, then made for the rear door, unlocked it.

Outside, in the trash of the alley, illumined by the faint starlight, he crouched against the brickwork of the cells for a moment, to get his bearings. He heard two more shots ring out from across the street.

Happy with that he padded past the corrals and waste lots behind the buildings fronting the main street, past the rats and scavenging dogs, then turned the corner at the first clear gap he came to. Stepping around more trash, he reached the street. From the cover of the corner of Hays Emporium he peered up the thoroughfare, towards the alley from where the shooting had been coming.

The next bit would be tricky. Using what dark shadow there was he sprinted across the street and into the alley opposite. No shots came his way. The ambusher must still be concentrating on the office.

The hairs at the nape of his neck now

prickling from keen anticipation, Scallon padded down the alley, then along the backs of the buildings on the bushwhacker's side of the street. At one place, startling him, a dog behind a high board fence set to barking, while viciously scratching at the wood that separated them.

He moved on quickly, until the barking ceased, but he found it had set his heart thumping against his ribs like a trip-hammer. Realizing his mouth was now as dry as desert dust he waited, gathering himself, before he moved on.

He finally came to the alley where he knew the rifleman was hidden. Here, he found the yellow street lighting was kind. It was casting a pale light into the mouth of the alley. And, yes, there he was, crouched against the building to the left and peering across the street.

Scallon blinked lids over bleak eyes. He must be a rank amateur. The dog's racket just now should have told him something, and the recent lack of fire from the office the rest. However, as if to partly contradict his suppositions, his quarry did now seem to be getting nervous. He was beginning to peer around, as if he was now starting to suspect things weren't right.

Hunched, Scallon padded up the weed-and-trash-filled alley, picking his way carefully. The rifleman did once stare down the dark maw, but Scallon was quick enough to freeze and crouch low enough as to be insignificant in the dark shadows.

He was near enough now to hear the ambusher cursing softly. And as if to express his growing frustration, he sent three shots towards the office.

Then Scallon noticed something odd. There were no people on the streets. It was late, admittedly. Maybe most folks were in bed and couldn't be bothered to investigate. Or they'd maybe guessed what was going on and were eagerly awaiting the result. Maybe some even wanted him dead.

He was right up on the man now. He dug his Colt into the small of the rifleman's back.

He hissed, 'One bad move, you're dead.'

The bushwhacker let out a startled gasp. He dropped the rifle as if it had grown hot and shot his hands skywards.

Scallon frisked the man for other weapons. There were none. He picked up the rifle. 'Make for the office, mister,' he growled.

The rifleman stiffened. He was about five-feet eight inches tall. Slim build. Fact was, he looked little more than a boy. When Scallon prodded him again, the rifleman started the walk, stiffly, across the broad thoroughfare. A few people were now venturing out of John's Place to peer his way.

In the office he pushed the man into a corner. 'Stand real still,' he said. He propped the man's rifle against the wall behind the swivel chair, then, splitting his attention between the man and what he was intending, Scallon thumbed a match into life and rekindled the lamp. In the amber light that flooded the office, he stared at the bushwhacker.

He was barely eighteen, at a guess. There was something vaguely familiar about the youthful features, but Scallon couldn't put a finger on it.

'What's your name, boy?' he demanded.

The youth stared defiantly. 'Elias Hagler.'

For Scallon, the whole thing slotted in immediately the name came. 'I see. So you figured to kill me, because I had a hand in killin' your brothers, that it?'

Hagler shuffled, looked at the office floor.

'You want to ride the same trail as Ben and your other brothers, boy?' Scallon rasped.

The boy shook his head. 'No, I don't.'

Scallon nodded. 'That's the way *I* heard it. But you figured you had to do something. Like take revenge … right?'

Hagler began to look more uncomfortable. He fiddled with a button on his threadbare coat. From under his worn slouch hat, sandy hair poked. Freckles spotted his sallow face. Down showed through the acne on his chin.

'Ben was no good, Elias,' Scallon went on quietly. 'He'd raised his hell and finally run out of luck. In the end he knew a rope awaited him in Rutland, so he pulled a gun on me. I didn't want to kill him, but I had to. There was no other way.'

Anger flared in the boy's eyes now. 'You could have backed off, not gone chasin' him into the mountains ... let him go.' A kind of vague hope flared up in Hagler. He added quickly, 'Ben was goin' to make a new life. He tol' me that before he left the ranch the last time.'

Scallon shook his head slowly. 'Not Ben, Elias. It had got too deep in his blood. He'd just have to keep on doin' what he did until he either ended up on a rope or finished the game the way he did ... through gunsmoke.' Scallon stared across the intervening space between him and the youngest Hagler. 'You're different, boy,' he said. 'You've got your whole life ahead of you. Don't make the same mistake your brothers did. None of them would've wanted you to do that.

An' gunnin' down an officer of the law is a hangin' offence.'

Elias looked distinctly ill at ease now. He stared worriedly away into the night beyond the shattered office window.

'Does your ma know about this?' Scallon asked. Elias shook his head. 'So, what about her, boy? Don't you think she's had enough pain?'

Elias stared defiantly. 'I reckon Ma would want this,' he blurted.

'You full sure about that, boy?' Scallon went on calmly. 'An' even if she did, you're the man in the house, don't forget that. You've allus known your brothers were wrong, and have resisted them. That alone makes you a tall man right off. You goin' to throw all that away?'

It was as if a dam had suddenly been opened in Elias. 'They never wanted me with them, not as I wanted to go!' he blurted. 'It was the war. They'd all been in the war. Ma said they came back bad – full o' hate, not her boys at all any more.

Because Ma had me late, I was a good ten years younger than Jim – who was youngest, 'til I came along. When Pa died two years ago, Ma said it was because his heart had finally been broken by them.' The young Hagler faltered. 'Well, it all fell to me then. Somebody had to take up runnin' the spread. Soon as my brothers started that crazy rustlin', I tol' them to stop grazin' their stolen cattle on Bar H land. Well, sir, I was plumb amazed when they did as I asked. Ben said it was because they didn't want to bring trouble on me. He said he wanted to see at least one Hagler go straight.'

'Good advice, Elias,' Scallon said. 'For Ben's sake, take it.'

He heaved himself away from the desk he'd been leaning against. He'd taken a few calculated risks in his life. This one had to be one of the most dangerous. He picked up the boy's rifle. It was an old Winchester, the sights worn. He crossed the office and handed it to Elias.

'This is one more decision you have to make, boy,' he said, 'maybe the biggest of your life. You can either use it, or ride out and make a real life for yourself and your ma.'

Elias took the gun and stared at it. After moments he raised his grey eyes and gazed at Scallon. Haunting indecision as well as a hint of – respect? – Scallon couldn't quite make up his mind which was the stronger – came to the boy's gaze. Then Scallon watched the youth lick his lips nervously, tighten his grip on the rifle until his knuckles showed white. He appeared to be trembling slightly now. His adam's apple travelled twice, up and down his scrawny throat. Scallon tensed, edged his hand towards his Colt. Don't be a fool, boy, he thought anxiously.

Then, abruptly, Elias thrust the rifle back into his hands. 'I won't be needin' that, Mr Scallon,' he said.

Scallon felt a deep wash of relief flood through him. 'You've just made the best decision of your life, boy,' he said.

Elias shuffled some more while shaking his head. 'I've been a damned fool, sir, an' you'd be right to jail me. Thing is, Ma don't know about this. Now she'll be waitin' an' worryin', wonderin' where I am. An' like you say, she's had enough pain. Don't suppose you can see your way to lettin' me go? Though, God's truth, I don't deserve it.'

Scallon stared at the boy. He wasn't usually a man to act on impulse, but this time....

'You're free, boy,' he said. 'Fortunately, no harm's been done.'

Elias's eyes rounded, mouth gaped a little before he closed it and his face set into hard lines. 'I'm beholden,' he said.

Scallon shook his head. 'You needn't be. Every man deserves one chance.'

'One more thing – I come to take Ben's body back,' the boy said.

'It's waitin'. Down at the barber's. Guess you'll have to knock him up.'

He watched the youngest Hagler step out

into the night. He must have a horse and wagon tied up somewhere, decided Scallon, and he exhaled a long sigh of relief as he let the tension fully drain from him. His knowledge of men told him Elias Hagler would not be coming back. He felt sure that there was one Hagler who would do his damnedest to make his way through life honestly.

Jenny Manners came in through the doorway as young Hagler stepped off the boardwalk. She paused there while she watched the lad cross the broad street. Then she gazed at Scallon with quizzical green eyes.

'I take it he missed,' she said dryly.

'Sayin' that, I guess you know him.'

'Huh, huh.' The emerald eyes roved his face once more. 'An' you let him go?'

'Had a little talk with him. He won't bother me any more.' He smiled at her. 'To change the subject, you didn't go back to the ranch.'

'Sometimes, your powers of observation

are quite overpowering, Mr Scallon,' she said mockingly.

Ignoring her sarcasm he said, 'Just figured you'd like to be there – Carder roaming free an' all.'

'The boys can look after things. Fuller's capable.'

'You sent a man out to the Circle M this afternoon.'

Jenny raised fine brows. 'You noticed. Well, I thought Fuller would need to know about Carder Randell.'

'You seem to place a lot of trust in that man.'

Jenny pursed generous lips. 'I pay him well to do a job.'

Then the urgent pounding of hooves distracted both of them. Jenny Manners frowned as she stared at him. 'Sounds urgent,' she said. 'Perhaps somebody for the doctor.'

Scallon paced out on to the boardwalk and stood gazing into the night, in the direction of the drumming hooves. Soon a rider came out of the gloom and pulled the bay he was riding to a slithering halt in front of him.

'Where's Ruger?' the rider barked harshly. His eyes were round and staring.

'Out of town,' said Scallon. 'I'm the law here at the moment.' But he found he couldn't take his eyes off the light bay horse the man was riding. He added, 'What's so damned urgent? An' what you doin' with Carder Randell's hoss?'

'Found him on the trail, near Scaggs Butte,' returned the panting rider, eyes wild. 'Been shot to hell.'

TEN

Scallon came down off the boardwalk. His stare was full of disbelief.

'Who are you, mister?' he rasped. 'What you doin' on the trail this time of night?'

Between gasps for breath, the rider spilled it. 'Will Jakes. Ride for the Jensens. Been looking for strays, when my hoss went lame. Was walkin' along the trail, hopin' for somebody to come by when I found Carder dead in the trees, at the foot of the butte. Used his hoss to get here.'

Scallon's gaze was bleak, his mind a turmoil. Who in the hell could've done such a thing? He stared in the direction Elias Hagler had taken moments ago. Well, he, more than anyone, had cause to want some, if not all, of the Randells dead, after the Wagon Wheel boss had done the bulk of the financing to help hunt down the Hagler gang. But he couldn't bring himself to believe it was young Elias. However, it had to be a possibility, no matter how improbable.

He began running after the boy. Elias had headed off down the street, in no great hurry, towards the east end of town. Scallon found the boy at a tie rail on the extreme edge of the settlement. He was undoing the halter that attached the scrawny roan mare to the shafts of a battered wagon.

'You'd better forget that fer a spoil, boy,' Scallon rumbled as he drew his Colt.

When he looked at Scallon, Elias's stare was round with incredulity; a frown registered his puzzlement. Then he looked at the gun.

'Thought we'd reached an understandin',' he said.

'That was before somebody rode in to report findin' Carder Randell dead on the trail.'

Elias's mouth dropped open. 'Carder

Randell?' Then he pointed a finger at his own chest. 'An' you think I.... Oh, my God, you've got to be crazy. An' hell, that'll set this range alight from end to end.'

Scallon nodded. 'That's why you're comin' with me.'

Elias stared. 'You can't figure I had anything to do with that,' he said.

'You came after me,' Scallon pointed out.

'I wasn't thinkin' straight,' blurted the youth. 'I'd come for Ben's body an' ... well, it was the idea of a man takin' money to hunt down another man that got to me. Didn't seem right. Still don't. But I realize that's the way things'll be, until they get changed for the better.'

'I gotta take you in, boy,' Scallon said. 'Mebbe it'll be for your own good.'

'What d'you mean?'

'Stimson Randell is goin' to be lookin' for answers. He's goin' to be thinkin' that maybe the last of the Haglers was lookin' for revenge an' gunned down his boy. When he finds you ain't at home, he'll be gettin' even more sure in his mind.'

Elias went pale. 'But that's crazy.'

Scallon nodded, grim-faced. 'Mebbe it is to you, boy. But to him it's a strong possibility. You'll be better off in jail, 'til cooler heads prevail.'

A glint of anger flashed in Elias's grey stare. 'But, so help me, I didn't do it.'

Scallon nodded. He even showed a hint of his twisted smile, though he accepted there was nothing remotely funny about the situation. 'I'm inclined to agree. I reckon you couldn't hit a barn door at ten paces with that Winchester you got. However....' He waved his Colt. 'Start an' move towards the jailhouse, Elias.'

The young Hagler hesitated a moment before reluctantly moving up the street. 'Ma'll be wonderin', worryin' herself sick....' he began before letting the rest of the words fade to silence, but their import was clear enough to Scallon.

'I'll get word, if I can,' he promised.

Glancing further ahead he saw Jenny

Manners was heading down the street towards him. When she drew close she stared at the young Hagler and said, 'You can't think Elias had anything to do with it.'

'He came after me.'

'But, that's ridiculous. He's–' Any more words just seemed to drain from Jenny Manners. Lost to her obvious disbelief.

'What?' rapped Scallon as he moved impatiently past her. 'Just a boy? He's a Hagler. Think about it, Miss Manners. You got brains.'

When he got to the office, he saw Carder Randell's bay was tied to the rail. He guessed the Crossed Keys rider who had brought the news had headed for John's Place. He'd looked in need of some liquid support.

Jenny Manners followed him to the jailhouse, the green satin dress she was wearing rustling loudly because of her impatient movements. Inside the law office, Elias hesitantly entered the cell Scallon allotted him, then turned and grabbed the bars as Scallon clanged the door to behind him and locked it.

'God's my judge, I didn't do it, Mr Scallon,' he said.

Scallon gazed at him. 'I told you, boy. I'm on your side.'

'Then why lock him up?' demanded Jenny Manners.

Scallon turned and stared into her green eyes, which he could see were now glinting like cut emeralds in the lamplight. 'You still ain't thinkin', are you? Until the dust settles, it's for his own safety.'

'Why, that's crazy,' she said. 'Nobody in their right mind will think Elias had anything–'

Scallon raised a silencing hand. 'Miss Manners, Stimson Randell virtually financed the whole of the hunting down of Ben Hagler and his brothers. Most said it had got to be an obsession with him. I know for sure the County's and Cattlemen's Association's contributions were small. Now this has happened Randell's bound to start looking in the direction of the Hagler ranch for answers, thinking revenge had to be the motive for the killin'. As you have explained to me, for all Carder's faults Stimson Randell loved his boy, to the point of foolishness, particularly after his wife died. And when a powerful man like Stimson Randell gets hit with the grief this news will cause, you can lay odds he'll start actin' crazy, even though he's normally a cool and calculating man.'

Jenny Manners looked at him, scorn on her pretty features. 'You are making a whole lot of assumptions, Mr Scallon, with no foundation at all.'

Scallon nodded gravely. 'I am, an' I hope to God I'm wrong, but somehow, I've a feelin' I won't be. But there's one thing that's got to be done, for sure. Carder's killer has to be found, an' soon.' He narrowed his gaze. 'You wouldn't have any ideas, would you, ma'am?'

To his mild surprise, Jenny Manners looked startled. 'Me?'

'Yeah. Things between you an' the Wagon Wheel ain't exactly all hunky-dory right now,' he said. 'Haven't been for some time, way I heard it.'

Sudden anger blazed into Miss Manners' eyes. 'Have you gone out of your mind? How dare you?' she demanded. 'Are you suggesting I had Carder Randell killed?'

The ferocity of the outburst sent a worm of suspicion burrowing like a weevil into Scallon, but why, exactly, he couldn't quite decipher. But such distrust had grown to be a part of him now, after long years of being on the sharp end of most forms of human deviousness, guile and plain untruthfulness.

He blinked lids over eyes that were chips of ice. 'Well, did you? You sent a man out to the ranch yesterday afternoon, or did you send him after Carder Randell?'

With that Miss Manners' temper seemed about to burst out into a blaze of verbal fire before she took a deep breath and calmed herself, though she was clearly shaking with anger.

'Now you are being ridiculous,' she breathed. 'I have better things to do than have neighbours gunned down.' Her green eyes kindled again and bright colour came to her lightly freckled cheeks. 'For God's sake – what for?'

He shrugged. 'You tell me.'

She let out a gasp and waved her arms to express impatience. 'Oh,' she blazed. 'This is ludicrous.' She stormed out of the office.

Scallon's grey stare followed her into the night. Maybe it was. Maybe it wasn't. At the moment, he could not close his mind to anything. And when the news got to Stimson Randell, as young Elias Hagler had said: this range would be set alight.

Well, he wasn't going to rush getting the news to the Wagon Wheel just yet.

He turned for John's Place. Inside, sure enough, he found the Jensen rider, Will Jakes. Whiskey seemed to have steadied him a little.

'Jakes,' he said. 'I want you to take me to the location of Carder Randell's body.'

Jakes pulled a face. 'Hell, do I have to?'

Scallon nodded, looked bleakly at the Crossed Keys rider. 'You do. Use Randell's bay.' He tossed a coin on the bar. 'Give the man another drink while I saddle my hoss.' He stared at Jakes, 'Be outside and mounted in ten minutes.' He went out and walked towards the livery. As he did Jakes bellied aginst the bar, waving his glass at the tired barkeep.

When he got to the stables and had roused the hostler Scallon said, 'Did Hank Ruger have a man who filled in for him while out on law business?'

'Jess Collier,' supplied the sleepy hostler. 'He's the town's constable.'

Scallon slipped the hostler a dollar. 'Could you see to it he covers the office while I'm gone? Got a prisoner in there.'

The hostler stared at the coin and nodded. 'Sure, Mr Scallon. Jess's allus glad of the extra cash.'

Scallon nodded, 'Good man, I'll take my roan now, if you please.'

ELEVEN

They arrived at Scaggs Butte soon after dawn. Scallon found it was a tall, gaunt rock with riven sides, yellowed now by the sun's early rays. Scallon saw that the trail on which Jakes had found Randell's body wound past the butte, then on through stands of ponderosa pine, down a long rocky slope and out towards the open country to the north. Jakes's lame sorrel was on a long rope nearby, cropping the grass that grew under the cliff. It didn't seem to be limping much now.

Scallon found Carder Randell's body still intact. No wildlife had begun to savage it, which he considered lucky. Inspection told him that Randell had been shot through the head and chest. From the look of them, either wound would have been instantly fatal. Whoever had done the job had sure intended to make certain Carder Randell never saw another day.

He turned to Will Jakes still up on the bay. 'How far is the Crossed Keys?'

Jakes waved a hand. 'Three miles. Over the ridge.'

'When I'm through, take Carder there. Don't want the coyotes to get to him.'

Jakes shrugged. 'Sure.' His brown eyes held Scallon's steely stare. 'You know what, mister? There's gonna be hell to pay soon as this breaks.'

Scallon nodded. 'It's been mentioned.'

He studied the way Randell lay, the hoof marks around him. Seemed when Carder had first been hit, the bay had reared and thrown him. The second bullet, through the skull, had knocked him flat. He'd never stood a chance.

Studying the angles, Scallon soon came to the conclusion that the shots must have come from the rash of rocks to the side of Scaggs Butte, maybe a hundred yards away from the body. At that range, a kill was almost certain for any competent marksman firing at an unsuspecting victim.

Scallon moved towards the rocks. He began a patient search. After minutes he found, behind a rock that gave good cover and a clear view of the trail, stubs of finished quirleys that had been ground into the bruised grass. And two shell cases. It was his guess that they came from a Winchester .45-70. A powerful weapon.

He searched further, the other side of the rock cluster. And there he found what he wanted to see. Hoof prints. He returned to Jakes, who was waiting and resting easy on the light brown bay, smoking and enjoying the sun's warmth after the cold night ride.

'OK,' he said. 'Take Carder. One more thing. After that, ride into Two Pines and wire Sheriff Boss Falster the bad news an' where to find the body.'

'Jensen won't like it,' complained Jakes. 'He likes his men working, not runnin' errands.'

Scallon stared. 'Then threaten him with Stimson Randell, damn it.'

Jakes brightened. 'Yeah. That oughta do it. An' after findin' this, I still need a drink.'

After watching Jakes ride off over the ridge, leading his now sufficiently recovered horse with Randell's body draped over it, Scallon picked up the hoofprints leading from the rocks. The trail took him around the foothills and across the southern edge of badlands. The rider, whoever he was, had been in a hurry and obviously knew the country. Scallon calculated that it would have been about dusk when Carder Randell entered the killing ground. The murderer must have had to make tracks through the dark.

Scallon travelled along the base of the benchland now, all the time scanning the ridges with an uneasy gaze. Though he wasn't anticipating trouble, based on the assumption that the bushwhacker would want to put distance between himself and his crime, he couldn't take chances.

Then the tracks disappeared into rocks. But before they had faded the bushwhacker had dismounted for a few minutes, had smoked a quirley, moved around a little, his boot marks mingling with the horse's imprints. The grim answer to the reason for the stop then came quickly. The bastard had put overshoes on the horse, to erase its tracks.

Cursing softly Scallon stared at the distances ahead. It had to be on instinct now. All this country was new to him, though he did recognize some features from the day before yesterday, when he and Hank Ruger had lit out after the killer of Jimmy Blue.

And that was another thing that had started to rankle with him, particularly now Carder Randell was dead. Though everything had pointed to the younger Randell – the light bay horse, the buckskin coat – it was beginning to look to be too obvious, too easy. Would Carder be damn fool enough to advertise the fact he was hurrahing Jenny Manners so openly? Even he had to have had more savvy than that.

Scallon rocked in the saddle. Doubt was starting to eat into him and once it did he knew it wouldn't leave him alone. It was down to his distrusting mind. And when he really started to think deep about recent events, analyse them, he felt that he may have been carefully manoeuvred in the direction of Carder Randell.

He stared ahead. The sun was climbing, beginning to burn. He took a draught of water from his canteen while moodily staring at the landscape that was beginning to shimmer with the growing heat. Thirst satisfied, he gee'd the roan forward once more – though he had nothing to follow – and began quartering the ground. It was a gamble, but at some point the man he was following would take off those overshoes and tracks would become obvious again.

Over long years he had built up this dogged determination, this philosophy of never giving up. Eight times out of ten it had eventually paid off.

A large stand of trees gradually came into view. He recognized them as the trees he had followed Jimmy Blue's killer into the other day, before those tracks, too, had petered out, only this time he approached them from the benchlands.

On a hunch, he struck off into them, rode past the cabin in the clearing. Soon he came out into a long, narrow valley. There, he saw full stockpens, branding fires, men working, beeves being marked. The acrid smell of burnt hair and flesh came to him on the breeze. Coon Valley?

'Hoist them, you sonofabitch!'

This harsh command came from behind Scallon. Stiffening, he did as he was bid, his mind working fast. It had to be a lookout, due to these troubled times. The rider came up behind him and pulled his Colt from its holster, then drew his Winchester from its saddle scabbard.

When he came round front, Scallon recognized him as one of the riders who had been with Carder Randell and Charlie Gratton, the Wagon Wheel straw boss, yesterday at the Circle M.

'No need for this, mister,' he said.

'You figure?' The lookout waved his Colt. 'Move on down to the brandin' area, hands high.'

Long before they reached the fires and pens, men stopped working to stare at them coming down the long slope. When in camp, Charlie Gratton stepped up to meet them. His stare was curious, neutral.

'Scallon?' He frowned. He turned to the lookout. 'What gives, Joe?'

'Came ridin' out of the trees. Figured you'd want to ask him a few questions.'

Charlie Gratton's gaze returned. 'Well, mister?'

'Drop my arms?' asked Scallon.

Gratton nodded. 'Go ahead. You can't be damn fool enough to try anythin'.'

Arms down, Scallon stared into the hawkish features of the straw boss. 'I won't mince words, Gratton. Carder's dead.

Bushwhacked at Scaggs Butte, sundown yesterday far as I could make out. Trailin' the sonofabitch that done it.'

Gratton stiffened. Eyes like chips of steel peered up at Scallon. The straw boss seemed to be having difficulty taking the news in. After moments he breathed, 'Carder?' Then his face set into menacingly grim lines. 'This some kind of sick joke?'

'No joke, Gratton,' said Scallon, his look sombre. 'Wish to God it was.'

'What the hell was he doin' at Scaggs Butte?'

'You don't know about Stimson bailin' him out?'

Gratton shook his head. 'Naw. Rode into the Wagon Wheel an' told Randell what you done. He said he'd handle it and sent us straight back to here, to Coon Valley, to finish the brandin'.'

Scallon gazed at the straw boss intently. 'Well, I won't beat about the bush. As a lawman acting for the county, there's things I have to know, an' I want them straight,

Gratton. Was Carder here with you the other day, all day, like you said?'

Gratton scowled, as though he resented the suggestion that he'd been lying.

'What you got was the truth, Scallon. Carder was nowhere near Two Pines.'

Scallon scrubbed his chin. 'Then it had to be somebody dressed up like him. He always wear the buckskin coat, ride the light bay?'

'Kind of his trademark,' Gratton supplied. Then the man's whole demeanour altered, from guarded hostility to one of sharp curiosity. 'What you tryin' to say, Scallon?'

The manhunter rubbed his chin. 'I don't know. Just hunches.' He kept his gaze on the straw boss. Gratton seemed, slowly, to be growing interested. Scallon went on, 'How long has the trouble on this range been goin' on?'

'Nigh on two years.' Then, as if on impulse, Gratton hesitated, looked around him. He barked, 'OK, boys, git on with the brandin'.'

Scallon met the straw boss's gaze as it swung back to him. There seemed a questing, keen intelligence in his probing look now. Gratton waved a gloved hand. 'Climb down, Scallon. Walk with me.'

Curious, Scallon did as he was bid. When they'd gone a distance from the branding crew, he said, 'You got somethin' on your mind, Gratton?'

The straw boss looked long and hard at him. 'You really after that killer?'

Scallon nodded. ''Til hell freezes over, if necessary. That's the way I am.'

Gratton nodded. 'An' that fits with the boss's opinion of you,' he said. He paused, his gaze long and searching, as if making up his mind about something. Then he said, 'Two years ago, Carder went off the rails. Claimed he was sick of Stimson continuin' to treat him like a child. But it all really started after Jenny Manners had refused to marry him. They'd kind of been childhood sweethearts, though you wouldn't know it now.' Gratton heaved a sigh. 'Well, he was gonna show that bitch, he claimed. Secretly, he got a bunch of rowdies together and began rustlin' the Circle M. Eventual result of that was John Manners got hit in the leg when he came upon them runnin' off some of his herd, though he never knew it was Carder.'

'An' Manners died,' said Scallon.

Gratton stared, hard. 'Was some ham-handed sawbones finished him, not the wound, but it was enough to jolt Carder out of his stupidity. He thought a lot of John, though he was rustlin' him. He had this crazy notion he was gettin' back at Jenny for refusin' him.'

'What happened after that?' said Scallon.

'He stopped the rustlin' right off, tol' his father what he'd been doin' a month or two later. That's when Stimson tol' me and set me to keepin' an eye on him.' Gratton stopped. His gaze turned brittle. 'That crazy kid ... dead? Still can't believe it.'

'Where does the Hagler gang come into all this?' pushed Scallon.

Gratton raised long, narrow brows. He growled, 'That bunch of no good sons-ofbitches? They started operatin' fourteen months ago, though it wasn't known it was the Haglers doin' the thievin' until Stimson Randell rode straight in on Bar H land one day and found Wagon Wheel beeves there, waitin' to be moved out of the country.'

'Elias told me he'd asked them not to,' Scallon said, 'and they'd agreed to steer clear of the ranch.'

Gratton shook his head. 'Well, they must've been cheatin' on the kid, or he asked them after the incident.' He waved a ham-like hand. 'No matter. That time the Haglers claimed the beeves'd strayed on to their land, that they were goin' to return them an' Stimson gave them the benefit of the doubt. But the rustlin' continued. We went on to Hagler land several times after but always found nothin'. Then they were caught redhanded, runnin' off stock. Though the gang escaped, they'd been identified. Straight off, a posse was formed.

The one you rode with. I guess the rest you know.'

'The Haglers are dead,' said Scallon. 'Who'd want to kill Carder now?'

Gratton's stare grew cold. 'Not all dead,' he growled. 'Like you say, there's Elias. Why, that low down sonof–'

'I got Elias in Two Pines jail, on suspicion,' cut in Scallon. 'But all the sign I found rules him right out. Whoever done this came this way, an' when I pick up his trail agin, I'll have him.'

Gratton drew himself up. Scallon could see there was now murder in the straw boss's eyes. 'By, God, I'll get the boys. We're comin' with you, mister. That crazy son of a gun meant a lot to me, though I of'en griped about him.'

Scallon raised a hand. 'Like to do this one alone, Gratton. Work better that way. One man on a horse ain't goin' to throw a scare into who I'm followin', but a crowd will. An' he's cute, slippery. He'll be hard to run down. I've a feelin' a posse'll force him clear of the country for a spell, an' that will prolong things, allow what's goin' on here to quiet down, an' the dust to settle, 'til folks won't be so keen.'

Gratton growled, 'But, God damn it, that sonofabitch, whoever he is, wants hangin' from the nearest cottonwood!'

Scallon nodded. 'An' if I weren't a lawman right now I'd feel inclined to go along with that. But I figure he has to be workin' for somebody on this range an' will stay close to keep drawin' his pay. That fact has to be my chance.'

'But, this is the killer of Carder we're talkin' about,' snorted Gratton. His frustration showed as he paddled the ground with high boots, snorting.

Scallon gazed at the champing straw boss. 'Not easy for you, Gratton, I admit. But if you'd ride to the Wagon Wheel, explain to Randell what has happened and come back this way, I'll leave a clear trail for you to follow. Maybe, by the time you get to me, I'll have somethin'.'

Gratton snorted, clearly unsatisfied, 'But, God damn it!' Then he seemed to take a hold of himself. He stared for long moments, then nodded. 'We'll play it your way. Guess Stimson will agree. May surprise you to know, you're high in his esteem. That's why he sent for you. He knew damn well things weren't over yet on this range. Now, with Carder dead....'

Gratton shook his hawkish head. 'God knows what this news will do to him.' Then he said, gruffly, 'You're goin' to need your guns.'

As Scallon moved towards the camp with the straw boss he said, 'One more thing, Gratton. You see any riders this mornin'? Got this hunch he came this way.'

Gratton shook his head. 'No, but I'll ask the boys. Maybe they've seen somethin'.'

The lookout had. The rangy rider with the large adam's apple nodded gravely. "Bout an hour ago. Was ridin' the east ridge.' He waved an arm vaguely to his right, at the rim of the valley. 'On'y showed hisself fer a second or two. But I see'd him. I ain't one fer missin' much.'

Scallon felt a thrill of anticipation, before he suppressed it. He'd never been one to build his hopes up on happenstance. But it helped keen him up again, shed some of his feelings of tiredness, for the sleepless night was beginning to tell.

He took Gratton's offered coffee and beans before he climbed on to the roan and headed for the east ridge.

TWELVE

Gaining the top of the ridge Scallon began patiently to quarter the ground again, for there were still no tracks, despite the sighting. And that fact pointed to the man he had been following, because of the sighting by the Wagon Wheel lookout. He began picking up little clues, while making steady progress north. The country was becoming more familiar to him. The hills ahead were the hills into which Pershay Canyon cleaved its way, and where Jenny Manners had her well-stocked ranch, though it wasn't visible just yet.

He was searching a stand of ponderosas when he found the tracks again. Had to be his quarry. All the clues pointed to him. Another quirley butt ground into the grass, the greenery pressed down by riding boots.

Then, as if by magic, clear tracks of a shod horse once more.

He stared in the direction they went; straight into the hills and no effort being made to cover them. It gave Scallon the comfortable feeling that the man he followed was assuming he'd thrown off what pursuit there might have been and he could now ride easy.

An hour later he came to a plateau, then to the lip of what he recognized to be Pershay Canyon. He stared into its wide green depths, at the sparkling silver ribbon of the stream flowing past willows, alder and aspens, then on past the adobe ranchhouse – a white speck in the distance. Fine cattle country. John Manners had picked well when he'd settled this land. Down there, even winter wouldn't be too much of a problem. Scallon found that the tracks he followed led him down to the canyon's entrance and on to the ranchhouse.

On the Circle M trail, he eased the roan to a halt, his face stone-like, uncertainty putting him in two minds. This didn't feel right. The tracks shouldn't be leading him to the ranch. It didn't make sense.

He slipped the retaining noose off the trigger of his Colt and urged the roan along the trail, right up to the ranchhouse. The squaw, Mary Plain Blanket and Drury Fuller, quirley drooping from his lipless mouth, were standing on the stoop, waiting and watching his progress as he came up the slope from the river.

At the tie rail Scallon climbed down. Fuller grinned, came down to him, talked past the quirley. 'Waal, howdy, Scallon. Hank's doin' jest fine, if that's what you're about.'

'Pleased to hear that.' Scallon looked around the outbuildings. 'You alone?'

Fuller nodded. 'Hands are out doin' whatever cowboys do.'

Scallon stared bleakly. 'I guess you wouldn't know about that.'

Fuller nodded, the grin still there. 'Right. Jest ain't my line of work.' He frowned now.

'You lookin' fer Jenny? She didn't come home last night.'

Scallon nodded. 'I know.'

'Then, jest what are you here for, Scallon?' Fuller even gave off a small, scoffing guffaw. 'Shouldn't you be about your lawful business, catchin' killers?'

'I am.'

Fuller's pock-marked face lost its smile. He frowned, furrowing his narrow brow. 'Now, jest what the hell you mean by that?'

'Mind if I take a look around?' Scallon said.

'Now, just why should I let you do that?' Fuller said. It was clear his sham good humour had gone. 'Miss Manners is the one you should put that question to.'

'You got somethin' to hide, Fuller?'

'I got nothin' to hide.'

'Then I'll take a look around.'

Fuller's draw was fluid and swift and took Scallon totally unawares. But it spoke volumes to Scallon. He stared coldly past the Colt at the mankiller.

Fuller said, his smile returning, 'On'y on Miss Manners say-so, Scallon. I've already tried to make that clear.'

Scallon realized his gut had clenched up. He'd heard of the deadliness of Fuller, the clinical way he did his killings.

'You goin' to shoot an officer of the law, about his lawful business, Fuller?' he said.

Fuller grinned disarmingly. 'Hell, no. Just ain't lettin' him snoop around without the boss's say so. She put me in here to look out for the place. I ain't about to mess up on a high payin' job. 'Course nothin' to stop you ridin' into town to ask, polite like.'

Scallon nodded. 'Might just do that. But before I do, you ain't no objections about me takin' a look in on Hank?'

'None at all, on'y it might give you ideas about jumpin' me.' Fuller's gaze now took on all the sincerity of a four-flusher. 'Now, I'm a peaceable man. Don't take easy to gunplay. So, to avoid trouble, I think it'd be wise if you jest rode on down to Two Pines, Scallon, an' see Miss Manners. She'll give you all the answers an' permission you need.'

Knowing that at the moment he was butting against a stacked deck, Scallon turned to the squaw. 'Mary. Deputy Ruger OK?'

The Indian shuffled, her face void of expression. 'Him fine. Sleeping now.'

Scallon nodded and climbed easily on to the roan. A veiled glance told him Fuller had lowered his Colt slightly, even relaxed a little as he was making to step back.

It had to be now, decided Scallon.

He rammed his boot heels into the roan's flanks. She reared, squealing as Scallon reined hard left. Her flailing hooves swung, beating the air close to Fuller's head, sending the mankiller staggering back and cursing and bringing up his sixgun.

Scallon drew his Colt and fired. His lead hit Fuller in the leg, knocking him off his feet. He fell heavily, jolting his weapon out of his hand. The mankiller's own shot went skywards.

Scallon was off his horse like a man gone berserk and running at Fuller. Reaching him he hammered the sprawled gunman, now howling his pain, over the head with the barrel of his Colt. Fuller yelled harshly then went silent, still and limp. Out cold. The dust between them began to settle almost immediately.

'Aayieee!' Scallon turned, startled, and found it was Mary Plain Blanket who had set up wailing. 'Aayieee!' she screeched again. A cold stare told Scallon she had her hands over her ears while she swayed to and fro. Then she began coughing as the acrid fumes from the guns began to get to her.

Leaving her to it, Scallon swiftly fished in his saddle-bag for his handcuffs, then pulled Fuller's slack arms behind him. Roughly, he secured them. Now he stared at the still wailing and coughing Indian.

'Quit bawlin' an fix his leg, Mary,' he shouted harshly.

She took her hands off her ears and waved them. Her eyes rounded. It was the first signs of animation Scallon had seen on her features. 'I do,' she wailed. 'I do. Damned quick.' She disappeared into the house.

Scallon stared about him, then at Fuller. The mankiller was still out cold and looked as though he might be for some time. Well, the large barns had to be first calls, Scallon decided. Because of the fuss Fuller had made, there must be something he had wanted hidden. He had to find it.

It proved to be almost too easy. The light bay was in a stall at the far end of the first barn. The only difference between this one and Carder Randell's bay was that the dark stockings didn't quite come as far up the legs – only noticeable when looked for. The discovery caused a warmth to fill Scallon. But there had to be more. A swift search led him to discover more evidence in a large bran bin. It was lightly covered with the meal. A buckskin coat, almost the same as Carder Randell's.

Jackpot.

Scallon decided he now had the man who

had hurrahed Jenny Manners' eatery and killed Jimmy Blue.

Now adding to his satisfaction, in the stall across from the bay was a sorrel that seemed to have been ridden hard recently. Nearby, a saddle was sitting over a saddle horse. Under the wooden frame, overshoes. And in the saddle scabbard, a Winchester .45-70. The rifle that had killed Carder Randell....? He drew it out, sniffed. Warm satisfaction filled him. It had been very recently fired. He replaced it. No wonder Drury Fuller didn't want him to poke around in the barns. It seemed he'd rode in on him before he'd got around to tidying up. Had the bastard been so confident that he thought he had shaken off any attempt to track him and could take his time about such vital matters?

Then, causing his gut to knot, the sound of a Winchester having a load jacked in came from behind him.

'Please turn around, Mr Scallon.' There was little doubt it was Jenny Manners' voice. 'Drury said I would find you here.'

Scallon's gut tightened. He turned slowly. She was standing just inside the barn. Her Winchester was to her shoulder, sighted right on his midriff.

'Don't be silly,' he said. 'Put that away, Miss Manners. There's a lot wants answers to be given to here.'

Jenny smiled sweetly, tilted her chin. 'I know. It seems you came a little too early, Mr Scallon. Your trailing skills really are commendable. Drury said he thought he had plenty of time to dispose of the evidence, thought nobody would find his trail until he saw you coming up the canyon.'

'Seems a man can guess wrong.' Scallon took a step forward. Jenny Manners tightened her grip of the Winchester and pulled it tighter into her shoulder.

'Stop right there. You know I can use this. Now, throw your gun over here and raise your hands.'

Oh, yes, he knew she could use it. But she

215

must have shot wide in Two Pines as Drury Fuller had run from the scene of his crime. With great care, Scallon did as he was bid. Hands now shoulder high he said, 'What's this all about, Jenny?'

Miss Manners raised her brows. 'Jenny now? Well, that won't buy you time, Mr Scallon. You must realize time's run out for you.'

Scallon shrugged easily, though he felt far from being at ease. 'Still like to know. Call it professional curiosity.' He licked bone-dry lips. Stall, he had to stall. There was always one mistake ... well, nearly always.

She was gazing at him. He saw her cold, round green eyes that held little suggestion that there could be some mercy forth-coming now, unlike the time she had granted him credit for his bath, hotel room and meals in Two Pines. When she spoke, her voice came out dull and metallic.

'You want to know, don't you?'

Was he starting to see a hint of well-concealed madness? He nodded. 'It'd help.'

She arched her pretty brows. 'Do you know our families wanted Carder and I to marry? Would you believe it? When I refused him he sulked, kept on sulking, even after I went East. I've learned since that he began rustling our cattle to feed his spite. He had some idea that doing that he would break us, just to get back at me. Finally Father caught his gang redhanded – though he wasn't with them – and he was shot.'

Her eyes glowed. A vague, almost whimsical smile flitted across her lips. 'I loved my father,' she said, her voice almost inaudible, 'beyond all else and I held Carder Randell responsible for his death. I hold Stimson Randell responsible, too, for spawning such a weakling. Now I've set out on a path to ruin him.'

'How?' said Scallon.

She put her head on to one side. A beam of sunlight spearing through a crack in the roof, highlighted her brilliant auburn hair. She giggled. 'How? I stirred up Hagler and his gang to start with, gave them information, allowed them to use Circle M range to hold cattle until they could be moved.'

Jenny Manners' stare darkened. 'But by hunting them down you killed that chance,' she said peevishly, 'so now I've set out to discredit the Wagon Wheel, starting with a man dressed up as Randell's stupid son, set him hurrahing Jenny's Eatery.' Her laugh was tinny, mocking. 'Can't you see how it would be viewed? The great Stimson Randell, stooping to bullying a feeble woman? Had you fooled, didn't it, until you came in here?' Then she added gleefull,. 'And I've got a lot more lined up for him.'

Staggering though it was, it was becoming clear to Scallon now that Jenny Manners was losing her mind, perhaps had been ever since her father's tragic death. Maybe that had caused it, though she appeared to have hidden it well. It now figured too, that her mind had become so twisted, so eaten with her hate and grief, that everything she was doing held a crazy logic, had a compelling rightness in it that was bringing her revenge for what had befallen her father.

'Why did you have Carder killed, Jenny?' he said.

She pouted behind the Winchester. 'He deserved it,' she shrilled. 'Has done ever since we were fourteen.' She paused, as if hesitant to relate what next she had in mind, then she went on, 'It was a high summer evening. We were by the pool we used to swim in, up the canyon. Sometimes we petted. Sometimes it got heavy, then he....' Her eyes flashed green fire as they riveted on Scallon. '...he took me, right there by the pool. *Took me.*'

She began wiping her hand down her rich dress, as if trying to wash something away. 'The filthy....' Her stare flashed as it snapped on to his. 'After that, I loathed him. He was so stupid. Can you imagine? Having a stupid boy like Carder Randell take *me?*'

Scallon saw Hank Ruger come round the doorway behind her, put his finger to his lips. He had a Colt in his hand. He moved silently. He looked pale and haggard. His

219

upper torso was naked, except for the bandages around it.

'Did Fuller kill Carder?' Scallon said.

She nodded. 'Of course he did. Now there's a man. A real man. He does as I ask. And, don't you see? With Carder dead, Stimson Randell has no heir.' She nodded eagerly. 'He'll die a broken man, I know he will.' She sighed. 'And Pa'll be looking down. He'll be smiling. His little girl ridding the range of his killer and the one that spawned him.'

Scallon swallowed on his dry throat. God, she was in an awful state. He gestured with a hand. 'Don't you realize you need help, Miss Manners?' he said, though he figured it was a damn silly question.

Jenny laughed, almost hysterically. 'Me, Mr Scallon? No, *you* need help. Now you know too much. There can only be one end for you and it is this.' She pulled the rifle into her shoulder. 'I can't allow you to stand in my way now I've got this far.'

Scallon was diving sideways and rolling

through the straw as Hank moved. The lawman came up behind Jenny, wrenched the gun from her hands just as she fired. The bullet went harmlessly wide.

Hank threw the weapon across the barn, then went back on his heels and leaned against the barn door, face ashen, holding his chest as Scallon picked up his Colt.

'Couldn't see her kill you, pardner,' Hank gasped weakly. 'You shootin' Fuller woke me. Came to the window. Watched you go to the barn. Then Jenny came along in her gig, talked to Fuller while Mary was fixin' his leg. Saw her pull her rifle from that scabbard she has on the gig an' head your way. With Fuller goin' nowhere, I figured the on'y thing to do was to buy in.'

Distracting Scallon now, Jenny Manners sank to the earth floor, began moaning. Then she set to screaming, beating the ground with her fists and shaking her head. It was as she did that the thunder of many hooves came from outside.

There was muffled talk, then Charlie

Gratton, Stimson Randell and half a dozen Wagon Wheel hands came to the barn door, Colts raised.

Scallon stared bleakly at the stocky rancher, at the fat cigar jammed in the side of his thick-lipped mouth, at the fierce glare in his slate-blue eyes.

'It's over, Randell,' he rasped. 'An' you owe me a thousand dollars.'

It turned out Mary Plain Blanket had made the buckskin coat Fuller used to impersonate Carder Randell, the light bay horse had been bought in especially for the job. Nobody blamed Mary Plain Blanket. She was just doing what she was told to do. It had meant nothing more to her than that. But, surprising Scallon, under her care, Hank Ruger soon recovered from his wound and, within a month, had resumed his duties.

Stimson Randell stopped the lynching the boys had had in mind for the killer of Carder. For all the younger Randell's faults, it became apparent to Scallon he had been popular with the hands and that they considered it was what Fuller deserved.

Drury Fuller was eventually tried and publicly hanged before the courthouse in Rutland's main square. To follow the hanging, a rifle shoot was organized and three horse races. Betting was heavy. A travelling fair was also brought in. It had a fine carousel.

Ironically, the loss of his son in the cleaning up of the range won Stimson Randell a heap of sympathy and a pile of votes when the time came for the election and with them the fruition of his dream – the governorship of the Territory.

Jenny Manners, blank-faced and vacant staring, had not spoken a word since her arrest. The trial was a farce. She was committed to an asylum for the criminally insane. A place was found near her sister Sarah's home in St Louis. Her sister had pleaded for it to be so. Stimson Randell had, with great magnanimity, agreed to the transfer. To pay for her comfort and welfare the Circle M had been profitably sold to Stimson Randell.

But long before most of those events occurred, Scallon had gone over the ridge above Rutland and towards the far away hills.

Oh, both Falster and Randell had asked him to stay on, but somehow he had been so sickened with events that he had declined. In any case, he still had the three promising dodgers Hank Ruger had offered to him. Chasing them up would keep him busy for quite a spell and perhaps they would help to take his mind off the harrowing events recently past.